LINDSAY PAIGE

MAKE ME

ME

fall

Cardinal
Point

First edition: January 2026
Library of Congress Cataloging-in-Publication Data

Paige, Lindsay
Make Me Fall (a Cardinal Point novel) – 1st ed
ISBN: 978-1-962174-11-4

Chapter One

Melanie

"What the fuck are you doing?"

The stepladder, which I balance precariously on as I hang purple and orange lights on my house to prepare for Halloween, wobbles even more when the sexy, annoyed voice of a man snaps the question at me. Ignoring whomever as I'm *so* close to finishing this section, I lift onto my tiptoes, wishing once more I had a true ladder.

That's when I lose my balance with a shriek. I wait for the brutal impact of slamming into the ground. Instead, strong arms snag me, and I'm held against a delicious-feeling body. He sets me on my feet, and I swivel to find my yummy neighbor. My heart hammers in my chest at the furious look on his face.

"I asked what the fuck you're doing," he repeats slowly as if I'm too stupid to understand what he said the first time.

"Isn't it obvious?" I ask, my hands moving to my hips. I'm not sure what he's doing over here. He sticks to himself, even though I wish he wouldn't because he is a seriously fine human being. Considering I have a boyfriend, I

1

shouldn't have thoughts like that. He's just too gorgeous to ignore completely.

His hair is cut in a bit of a fade from his time in the military, which I'm assuming because of the sticker on his truck. His beard is trimmed, and it nearly touches his chest. Brilliant, pissed-off blue eyes stare at me. Full lips press into a firm line. I wish he'd grab me and kiss me.

"That you're being stupid, yeah."

I snap out of my ogling. "I'm not stupid," I grit.

"Then why are ya standing on top of a damn stepladder, balancing on your fuckin' toes?"

"Because it's all I've got!" I retort, exasperated and wondering how someone so hot can be such an ass.

"Next time, if you need a fuckin' ladder, ask and you can borrow mine."

"I would've been fine if you hadn't come over and startled me," I point out. "I don't need your help."

He raises an eyebrow at me. We stare at one another in some sort of standoff, with me thinking I'd rather have fallen and busted my ass than have him in my yard.

His lips twitch as if fighting a smile, and he says, "You wanna go somewhere with me tonight?"

My jaw falls open at the surprising change of topic and the audacity of this guy. He's inviting me out after he just called me stupid? Is *he* stupid? "You're asking me on a date?" I ask him incredulously.

He shakes his head. "I'm going out with some friends, and there's someone I think you should meet."

I frown and furrow my brows, confused. "You're setting me up on a date? I have a boyfriend."

Again, he simply shakes his head. "You coming or not?"

If it's not a date, then what the hell is it? Curiosity

makes me want to go, but I can't help saying, "Did anyone ever tell you that you're an asshole?"

His smile sends the air whooshing out of my lungs. God, he's breathtaking. "Only every other day. Austin Lowe," he says, holding out his hand as he supplies me with his name.

"Melanie Fields," I return.

"You look like a woman who likes to take her time gettin' ready, so you've got an hour and I'll be back to get you."

I stare at him, dumbfounded. I never said I'd go, did I?

It doesn't matter. I have to go.

I've been intrigued with my neighbor ever since I moved in and first caught sight of him. He has a story. I have no idea what it is, and I have a feeling it's not pretty, but damn if I don't want to know it. My boyfriend once again ditched me tonight, so I might as well have some friendly fun if I can.

"Go," he orders with a nod toward the entrance to my house.

My legs turn to carry me inside before I have the chance to think twice about it. I shower, shave, fix my hair and put on makeup, and it's as if I'm on autopilot the entire time. When I walk back out my front door with five minutes to spare, Austin is walking to his truck as I cross my yard to his.

"Where are we going?" I ask as he opens the door for me.

"The Mad House," he replies, referring to Cardinal Point's one and only bar in town.

As he backs out of his driveway, I glance over at my place. My lungs still as I see my house is covered in lights. I had up only one strand of lights and now the rest are installed.

"Did you do that?" I ask softly.

3

"Yeah."

Clearly, he's faster at hanging lights than I am.

"I could've done it." There's no bite in my tone, but I'm compelled to say it anyway.

"Think you established you could, but I didn't need you decidin' not to ask to borrow my ladder, so I threw the rest of 'em up before I took my shower."

I don't remember the last time anyone did something considerate of me without my asking while also realizing I *could* do it myself. Or when someone did a nice thing for me, without the motivation being that they didn't trust in my capabilities to do it myself.

"Thanks," I mutter. "I'll find some way to repay you."

"No need."

The thing is, I'm practically conditioned to return the favor afterward. Maybe conditioned isn't the right word. Still, I can't help but want to show I appreciate his assistance, even if I didn't need or want it. Maybe especially because I didn't need it and he went out of his way like everyone else.

I feel I should say something, inquire more about who he's taking me to meet, but I can't bring myself to speak. Maybe it's because he was nice to me after being so rude. Or maybe it's because his truck smells of him, and I'm embarrassed that I'd like to live here now.

Luckily, the drive to the bar is short, one of the many perks of living in a small North Carolina town. Cardinal Point might not seem like a lot to most, but it's ours, and I love it here. Even if everyone knows your name—and your business.

The Mad House is located on Main Street, which is lined with brick buildings that have been here for ages and ages and houses various businesses. The town seems to have an unspoken rule that if you open a business in downtown Cardinal Point, its name should incorporate a pun. I'm not sure exactly how The Mad House got away with breaking the rule.

I'm quiet as we drive past various businesses, like Bake My Day, The Chair Necessities, How Hardware Could It Be, and one of my favorite diners, Go Ahead and Fry Me. The diner is run by Mrs. Edna and Mrs. Mille, two old ladies who are the best of friends, mother hens for the young folk in town, and entertain us all with their bickering. Everything they serve puts everyone's grandma to shame.

And then there's The Mad House. My favorite part of the bar is the walls, which are covered with photographs. I'm not sure how the tradition of pinning photos to the walls after someone has passed started, but Cardinal Point's most beloved residents live on in the photos scattered within.

As we park, I marvel again at how Austin has kept to himself enough that I have never heard any gossip about him. Something tells me the moment we walk into The Mad House together, rumors will spread. Too soon to tell if the reaction will be positive or not. Likely a mixture of both.

I brace as Austin holds the door open and I walk inside just ahead of him. It's busy as usual with folks at their favorite tables, playing darts or pool, or hovering near the old jukebox to choose the next song. Since I don't know exactly why I'm here, I pause until Austin can lead the way.

Everyone seems to glance over at us, and sure enough, the murmurs start when they realize I came with him. Austin doesn't seem to notice. He stalks over to a table already brimming with people, and I follow along like a lost puppy.

The group quiets as we approach. Austin places a hand on my lower back, with such a light graze I feel as if he's

5

trying *not* to touch me, and nudges me forward. I take a step to stand next to him, and the bit of heat from his fingers falls away, leaving unfounded disappointment in its wake.

"Amelia, this is Melanie. Thought you should meet," he says, addressing the only girl at the table. Wait. He brought me to meet a *woman*?

Her eyes widen in surprise, but she scoots further into the booth and pats the spot next to her. I take a seat, utterly confused and uneasy at being thrust into this group when I have never met anyone here before. Why did I come again?

"What do you drink?" Austin asks, still standing at the end of the table.

"Amaretto sour?"

He raises an eyebrow at me. "Are you sure?"

I nod once more; his lips twitch as if he's fighting a smirk. He turns and walks off to the bar.

"How do you know my brother?" Amelia questions.

Wait, he brought me to meet his sister? What the hell is happening here?

"He's my neighbor," I answer.

She nods as if that somehow makes sense. "I don't have a lot of girlfriends." At this, I look around the booth again. "He's playing matchmaker with us; apparently, he thinks you'll make a good friend."

Interesting. Because Austin doesn't know me. Before I can question her further about her brother, he returns with my drink and a beer for himself. That's the last acknowledgement I receive from him. He talks to the others around the table. He grabs me fresh drinks when my glass runs low, but otherwise, I'm left to talk to his sister.

She, I learn, is a librarian at one of the local schools. She's the same age as I am—twenty-five—and she and her brother aren't originally from the area. When Austin steps away with one of his friends to play pool, I can't help but ask the question burning on the tip of my tongue.

"What's his deal?"

"That's a tale for another day, but long story short, he has gotten screwed over more times than I can count. These guys here are about the only people he lets get close anymore. They all served together and work either for Austin or with Silas. I only got to barge into their group because, well, it's what I do. I'm kick-ass, and it helps I'm Austin's sister. Kinda shocked he brought you, honestly."

"Apparently, it's because I'm too stupid to be left to my own devices," I reply dryly. When Amelia gives me a questioning look, I recount how I came to find myself at The Mad House with her.

"Interesting," she comments.

Is it? Just as I slurp the last of my drink, Austin appears to drop another one off along with a bottle of water before returning to the pool table. I guess four is my limit.

"How long have you known him?" Amelia asks.

I frown at her question. "I mean, he's been my neighbor for like a year, but today's the first time I've talked to him." Her brows raise in surprise. Before I can ask her about it, Austin appears at the table again. His body coils tight with tension.

"Let's go," he snaps at me.

"What's wrong?" Amelia inquires, her gaze searching the patrons of the bar. She spots something that makes her frown. "Austin, you don't have to leave."

"Melanie." My name is an explicit order, and I scramble to stand. Amelia reaches out to snag my wrist, though.

"Austin," she tries again. "You shouldn't let her run you off."

Her? Who are they talking about?

7

"Mel has to be up early tomorrow for work." I look over at him, surprised he paid attention to me enough to know my shift schedule. Austin grabs my elbow and leans across me to place a kiss on his sister's cheek. My breath stills in my lungs as his body heat warms me all over. Just as quickly, it's gone, and he pulls me away.

We're almost to the door when a woman steps into our path. She's the opposite of me. As skinny as a stick, with blonde hair and hazel eyes in vast comparison to my black hair, green eyes, and more curves than I care for honestly.

Austin's hand tightens on my elbow for a split second before he wraps an arm around my waist and tugs me half a step back from the woman so I'm slightly behind him.

"It's nice to see you're moving on, Austin," she says. "But I hope you don't think I'm letting her anywhere near our daughter."

Wait. *What?* How many times will I have to endure whiplash tonight? Austin has a kid! How have I never seen him with her? She is clearly the *her* mentioned moments ago and the reason we're heading out early. An undercurrent of fury seems to vibrate within him just by being in her presence. Or maybe because she approached him and assumed I'm with him?

"We're not talking about this now. Get the fuck out of our way," Austin snaps at her. I thought he sounded pissed earlier when he caught me on my stepladder. That's nothing compared to the venom in his tone now. I sure wouldn't want to be on the receiving end when he's truly angry.

She must be used to it, though. She smirks at him and then smiles at me in such a manner it's like she's baring her teeth. I'd bet my paycheck she was a total mean girl in high school. She steps to the side, and Austin pulls me the rest of the way out of the bar. He says nothing as we get into the truck.

A glance into his backseat reveals that, sure enough, there's a car seat back there. I have so many questions, I'm unsure which I'd want to start with. All of them seem intrusive. I'm almost afraid to talk. The hostile air inside the vehicle doesn't help. I don't want to be the one to break the silence, so I remain quiet.

Austin seems lost in his own headspace. So much so that when he parks in his driveway, his truck idles for two minutes without him making any move to exit or even turn the vehicle off.

"Thanks for introducing me to your sister," I force myself to say.

Austin doesn't acknowledge I've spoken, so after a few seconds, I open the door and hop out to rush home. It's probably best I forget my entire interaction with Austin this afternoon.

Once inside, I change into an old, oversized T-shirt and wander into my kitchen, feeling like I need coffee.

Noticing the trash needs to be taken out, I pull the bag from the bin while the coffeepot gurgles to life. As I face the back door, I spot it. A scream cuts through my throat as the bag falls. As if the floor is lava, I jump onto the counter and cry out again as the terrifying being takes a step.

"Melanie!" A second later, Austin rushes into my kitchen. He pauses upon seeing me crouched on my counter. Carefully, like I'm a scared animal backed into a corner and I might run or bite at any moment, he walks over and braces his hands on either side of me. "What..." He tilts his head and starts again. "Why are you screaming?"

I grab his shoulders, turning him toward my back door, and stretch my arm to point at the intruder. I shriek once more at more movement, my fingertips digging into his skin. Austin follows my gaze, and it takes a second for him to locate the minor source of my terror.

And then, he *laughs*.

A full-belly, hunched-over laugh that stuns me for a moment. Who knew he could get even more gorgeous?

"You're over here screamin' bloody murder over a damn *frog*?"

I scowl at him. "I don't do snakes, frogs, spiders, or lizards. That cursed thing has me trapped!"

He laughs again, turning to face me. He does another sweep over my body. I realize then that I'm in only a T-shirt and because of my position, he can probably see my panties. I tug my shirt over my knees to cover myself better as he lifts his gaze back to mine.

"Well?" I snap, annoyed.

He smirks and raises an eyebrow. "Is that your way of asking me to get rid of the frog for you?"

At his question, I lose all attitude. "Will you?" I ask hopefully. That would be the most convenient solution for me.

Austin smiles full-on at me now. He's the most handsome man I've ever seen, celebrities included. "I thought you were a strong, independent woman, who doesn't need anyone's help."

I scowl. He's also the most annoying man I've ever met. "I don't need *your* help."

"Then what are you gonna do about the frog?" he asks with laughter in his tone. His amusement with me is such a stark contrast to the mood he was in not even five minutes ago.

My gaze flicks back to the tiny green creature. Either I gather some courage to knock him down with a broom and throw him outside or call my father or one of my brothers. I could try Tyler, but he wouldn't come for this; I know because I've called him before.

I can handle many things on my own, but I shudder at the thought of getting any closer and risking that thing jumping on me. Calling for help is a must in this situation. Honestly, I'm leaning toward my dad. He would give me the least amount of shit for not wanting to be near the monster. But I'm not telling Austin that. It might be nearly midnight, but Dad would still rescue me.

"Just leave," I order with defeat. No way am I calling for help in front of him.

Austin stares at me for a moment and then turns, picks up my trash bag, and heads for the back door. He nabs the frog, opens the door, and disappears, taking my garbage with him. Within a minute, he returns and glances at me as he washes his hands.

"Thanks," I squeak, relaxing enough to rest my butt on the counter and let my legs dangle. My eyes fix on his hands. Something as simple as his palms moving together as he cleans them fascinates me, causing me to wonder what they would feel like.

God, that is so inappropriate. I clear my throat and finally look away as he dries them. The silence looms around us again; this time, I break it.

"Will you give my number to Amelia? I didn't exchange numbers with her." Meeting her may be the highlight of my night. She seems to have a personality that is just so unapologetically her, and I'd love to become friends with her.

Austin nods. I hop off the counter, snag a piece of paper from a notepad on the fridge and write it down. When he takes it, his fingers graze mine, and my breath stutters. A feather-light touch, and yet I *know* without a doubt those hands can do some deliciously dirty things.

"I'm next door if you need something. I'd rather you ask than get hurt doing something you shouldn't." With a hint of laughter, he adds, "Or die over the sight of a frog."

Part of me wants to argue with him. I wasn't doing something I shouldn't have been doing. Perhaps I was being a bit reckless, but that's none of his concern. And I wouldn't have died over the stupid frog.

I don't argue because my insides turn to mush at realizing this near stranger doesn't want to see me hurt. It feels nice and makes me feel pathetic at the same time.

"I'm gonna go," he says when it's clear I don't plan to respond to him. I nod and then Austin rushes out of my kitchen.

Finally, I've talked to my hot neighbor, and I almost wish I hadn't.

Chapter Two

Austin

All I saw yesterday when I came home was the nicest pair of fucking legs I've ever seen in my life. Now, I've spotted Melanie here and there since she moved in next door, but I try to ignore the sight of any woman. If it weren't for my daughter, my sister, and my mother, then I would declare all women inherently evil. Angela, my ex-fiancée, is the evilest of them all.

So, I avoid the opposite sex if I can. But seeing that long stretch of legs balancing on that stupid fucking stepladder, exposed thanks to a pair of shorts for a still-warm October, and I couldn't stop staring. Her recklessness also filled me with a surprising amount of anger. Even though I couldn't help but admire those shapely legs leading to maybe the best ass I've ever seen, I was unjustly pissed. Pissed even as she literally fell into my arms and I took in what easily had to be the most gorgeous woman on earth.

She can be the sexiest woman alive for all I care. I still don't want to take her for a roll between the sheets. Okay, I do, but I won't. I'm not gonna screw my neighbor for that to bite me in the ass. Spending more time with her helped ease that urge a little. She's infuriating. Her terror of a little green frog was hilarious, though.

"Daddy!"

I crouch and open my arms for my seven-year-old daughter, Erin, who runs full speed at me.

"Hey, baby girl." I wrap her in my embrace, enjoying her giggles as I twist and cause her legs to swing around. Catching sight of Angela barreling toward me as well, I add, "Why don't you head inside and figure out what you want to do today?"

She takes off the moment I set her down.

"Are you going to tell me who you were with last night?" Angela folds her arms over her chest expectantly, as if I owe her an explanation.

"It's not important."

She honestly isn't. Melanie is my neighbor who, after spending a few minutes with, I thought should meet my sister. Amelia complains all the time that she doesn't have enough girlfriends, and because she hangs out with the few friends I have, she's right. It seemed as though she and Melanie would get along. What can I say? They both have annoying qualities.

"She's the first person you've gone out with in years," she points out.

"It wasn't a date."

"Sure looked cozy."

"Is there something else you need?" I finally snap. "It's not like I'm introducing anyone to Erin." She opens her mouth, but I cut her off. "Great, thanks. See you Monday." I turn on my heels and storm inside, careful not to slam the door in her face.

"Daddy!" Erin shouts from the kitchen.

Her voice is enough to shake loose the tension from

speaking with Angela. I always thought people were full of shit when they said kids were the light of their lives. Erin proved it can be true. It's difficult, and I don't see her nearly enough, but she can still turn a shitty day around.

I make my way in there to find her resting her arms on the table, leaning forward to stare at the container of goodies. "Can I have a cookie?" Drool might as well from her mouth.

"Yeah."

"Did you make these by yourself?" she asks incredulously as she snags one. She examines it as if something must be wrong with it if I made it.

"No. They were a gift. What do you want to do today?" I ask, taking a seat at the table with her.

That's another thing. Melanie seemed completely thrown off that I'd help her, and despite telling her there was no need for repayment, she found a way. I was surprised to find the container of cookies on my front porch this morning with a note thanking me for disposing of the monster in the kitchen. Her words, not mine.

Erin hums. "These are great. Can we bake a pie today?"

"Sweet tooth still bothering you?"

My girl smiles. She loves sweets, and her favorite thing to do is bake. Angela made it so I only see her on the weekends, which has backfired on her. Mostly because whatever Erin wants to do, we do. And my daughter adores her daddy. She sees me as a hero, though I'm not. Angela can't stand how much Erin loves me.

"Are the cookies from your new friend?" Erin asks as I gather what we need to make a pecan pie, one of her favorites to bake.

I still and turn to face her, careful with my tone as I ask, "What friend?"

"Mommy said you had a new friend."

I will kill her!

"Mom was mistaken."

Erin frowns, but doesn't say more. If I *were* dating, the last person who should tell Erin is Angela. She's a freaking snake. If it weren't for Erin, if I never saw her again, it would be too soon.

Angela and I met during my time in the military. Stupidly, I thought she was different. While on my first deployment, there were so many guys who either cheated on their significant others or were cheated on. Angela was the exception.

Until she wasn't.

She was unfaithful to me while I was gone, but I'd already knocked her up. The only reason I know Erin is mine is that when we had custody papers drawn, a test confirmed it. Now, I'm unfortunately tied to Angela for the rest of my life, and I'd rather lose my balls than enter another relationship.

Erin and I make two pies and pretty quickly dive into one. When Erin asks what I plan to do with the other pie, I advise it will probably go to her aunt. With bellies full, my daughter decides she wants to draw. At some point, she wants to shop for Halloween costumes, so off we go.

I live for the weekends. To think my ex gets about three hundred days with Erin compared to my approximate sixty-five pisses me off to no end. Fighting her was tiresome. It seemed like no matter what I did, I couldn't win. My hatred for Angela started when I found out she cheated on me, but it was burned into every fiber of my being once it was declared I only get weekends with my daughter. Not even every weekend. Every other weekend.

If she wants to hate me back because I spoil my

daughter more than she does, tough shit. I've got a good kid still. One who behaves, is respectful, and doesn't act like a brat.

Our day is jam-packed with whatever Erin wishes to do, and by eight thirty, she's crashed in her bed. I'm cleaning up the kitchen when I glance outside and see the stupidest sight for the second time this week. Before I can think twice, I storm out my front door and over to Melanie's house.

"You said you aren't stupid, and yet here we are again."

Melanie startles and nearly falls out of the tree she's climbed into.

"Jesus, Austin. Why do you keep trying to make me fall?"

"You're in a fucking *tree* in the *dark* to decorate for fucking *Halloween*, Melanie," I point out the obvious.

"Well, we're already a week into the month, and I can't wait until I have daylight to do it," she argues.

"Get out of the tree."

She folds her arms across her chest and glares down at me. "Did I miss the part where you can boss me around in my own damn yard? It's been a long day, and I would like to decorate my house, so please leave me alone."

"Why are you even decorating?"

Melanie sighs as if I'm the most annoying person she's ever met. *Ditto, sweetheart.* "Because I find it incredibly sad that kids have to trunk or treat or whatever, and this makes me happy even if no one shows up. I mean, for God's sake, no other house in our neighborhood is decorated at all! You should all be ashamed of yourselves. Now, if it's not too big of an inconvenience to you, can I get back to what I was doing? As a kid, I climbed trees all the time with my brothers. I'm fine. I will not fall, so go back home."

She's not thrilled by my presence, yet I can't do as she's

asked. Her attitude turns me on entirely too much. There's also the matter of her not caring if she falls and breaks a leg, which bothers me more than it should.

"You're stressing the shit out of me." The admission surprises me, both that I voiced it and that it's true.

"Right back at ya."

I press my lips together to fight the smile that wants to shine her way. Why do I find her amusing?

Melanie ignores me and plucks something from the box she has balancing between two limbs. She hangs three bats around her. Next are some finishing adjustments on nearby faux webbing. She then grabs the container and lets it drop to the ground.

"Wait," I order when it's clear she's about to climb down. I don't even know how the tree is supporting her. Not that Melanie is a heavy woman, but the branches aren't that thick. Every movement she's made has them swaying. I'm sure she can jump down herself and be fine. Still, the need to ensure she safely makes it to the ground flares to life. "Let me help."

"I don't need your fucking help!" she snaps, a fury unleashing within her from out of nowhere. "I'm not incompetent. I'm not incapable. I'm not weak. I'm not helpless. I can do it my damn self!" Her voice rings out in the quiet night air. Her chest heaves as her grip strangles the poor tree. "I'm sorry it's an insult to your manhood that you aren't needed right now, but please, leave me the hell alone!"

Okay, then. I've pushed a button I didn't realize existed. And yet...

"I know you don't *need* my help, but it would make *me* feel a hell of a lot better if you'd allow me to assist. Please. Let me do this because it's something *I* need." That's the

God's honest truth, too. I don't know why I can't walk away and let her do this. All I know is that if I leave her here, I'll toss and turn until the next time I see her.

She stares at me for a moment. I lift my arms in one last silent plea just as she bends her knees and falls forward, her hands landing on my shoulders. The moment her weight shifts onto me, I slowly lower her until her feet are on the ground.

Like an idiot, I don't set her down a foot from me like a normal person. No, she's now barely an inch away. Her breasts brush my chest with every breath. Breasts I'm doing my best not to spare a glance at.

I can find a woman when I have an itch to scratch and I'm sick of my hand, but having Melanie against me like this? It feels like it's been entirely too long since I've been with a woman when it was just a month ago.

"Thanks," I mutter.

She takes a step back, and I grab the box she dropped before she can. She sends a glare my way, but says nothing as I follow her to the front porch.

"What do you have left to do?" I ask as I place the decor on a rocking chair and pull my phone to check the camera in Erin's room. I haven't yet managed to get rid of the baby monitor...just in case she happens to need me. My daughter sleeps soundly. I leave the app up and prop it on her windowsill so I can easily monitor her.

"Inflatables and my porch."

I glance down at the items left and then around her porch. "How do you plan to hang this shit?" I already know because the stepladder leans against the porch railing opposite where I stand. Where the fuck is this boyfriend she has? Or her father? Or her brothers? Literally anyone, so it's not me.

"Austin." She sighs my name as if I'm the most taxing person she's ever met. "It's been a long day," she reminds me. "I don't need my annoying neighbor up my ass about how unsafe I'm being while I decorate *my* house."

"I'm not stopping you. I'll help." We're both surprised by my response, and when she opens her mouth—likely to argue because what else would she do—I add, "You said it's been a long day. If I help, you'll finish sooner."

"Fine, but I need alcohol to deal with you." She disappears inside and returns a moment later with a glass of what I'd guess is an amaretto sour and a bottle of beer. She shoves it into my chest. "Maybe it'll make you more tolerable to be around."

My lips press together as I hold back a chuckle. My presence has never annoyed a woman like this. I don't think I've ever found an annoyed woman so cute. Melanie grabs some decorations and hands them to me, bossing me with her directions.

"What do you do for work?" I ask as I hang fake spider-webs in one corner.

"I'm a paramedic."

That explains her job schedule. Before I can process more than that, Melanie casually asks, "So you have a daughter?"

I can't help but grin. "Yeah. Erin. She's seven. She loved the cookies you left."

Melanie looks away as if she doesn't want to admit she clearly left the goodies. "I kinda feel bad that I've lived here all this time and didn't know."

I shrug. "You work weekends, and that's the only time I get to see her."

"I'm sorry."

The sincerity in her voice makes me pause. I glance over

to see her staring out over the yard. The hell if I want to push another invisible button. I keep quiet, and we work to deck out her porch until it's spooky and ready for the upcoming holiday.

"Do you like pecan pie?"

She nods.

"Be right back."

I jog over to my house, snag the extra pie, and return to find an empty porch, but the front door is still open. The screen door creaks slightly as I open it and step inside. What the hell? Not only has Melanie decked out the outside of her house, but Halloween exploded within as well. Ghosts, skeletons, pumpkins, and more. The decor is seemingly everywhere in her living room. When did she have time to do this?

My attention falls on the couch. I couldn't have been gone but a few minutes, but it was enough time for Melanie to plop down onto her sofa and fall asleep.

I drop the pie off in the kitchen and then return to Melanie. Should I cover her up? Take her to her bedroom? Leave her as is? With a silent groan, I lean down to pick her up. The idea of leaving her here when she's had a long day will nag at me all night. I'm not heartless.

Melanie doesn't stir as she moves from the couch to my arms. I walk down the nearby hallway until I find what looks to be her room. Her bed is a mess, the covers still askew from the morning. At least Halloween is limited to her living room and outside. I gently place her in her bed and cover her up.

God, she looks so peaceful and beautiful.

I've gotta get the hell out of here. I turn on my heels and hightail it out of there, locking the doorknob on my way out of the house. Melanie is hot and all, but I'm not interested in relationships, and something tells me having a quick fuck with my neighbor wouldn't exactly be the neighborly thing to do. *And she's got a boyfriend*, I remind myself. The last thing I need is to hang around Melanie.

I'm barely through the door at work the next morning before Stacey, my front desk clerk, appears with a mug full of coffee.

She holds it out to me. "Good thing I started a pot this morning. You look tired. Late night?" Her eyes search my face with an unreadable expression.

"No more than usual. Thanks." I lift the cup before taking a sip. Stacey making coffee for us isn't all that unusual, but this is the first time she's brought some to me. Her lingering in my office makes me shift my weight. Why is she still in here?

"Good weekend with Erin?"

I nod once. Personal matters aren't something I typically disclose at work with employees who weren't friends of mine first. There's a line in the sand, and while I treat my employees well, I've always been extra cautious where Stacey is concerned. She's our only female employee, and considering my history with women on top of that, I don't want her experience here to be anything but professional.

Again, she speaks. "Must be hard to have her only on the weekends. You're such a good dad, too." And how does she know that? Erin doesn't come up here much since she's primarily with Angela. I'm overthinking things. Stacey sighs and leans against the doorframe, shaking her head with an air of disbelief. "Some women don't appreciate what they have while they have it."

Yeah, that's the end of this conversation. "Thanks for the coffee. I gotta make some calls this morning if you don't mind."

"Oh, of course." She takes a step back. "Just a heads up, I reorganized your files in here. Your desk was getting messy, and I know you like things neat."

Now that she mentions it, my eyes rove over my desk. She did tidy up. I don't like that either. "Appreciate it, but no need to do anything in here. I'll handle it. Shut the door on your way, please."

She nods at my dismissal and finally leaves. I really hope she doesn't start making things weird. Finding a replacement would be a hassle. Before my thoughts can dwell on the topic longer—or worse, return to a certain pain in the ass neighbor—I turn my computer on and make those calls.

Chapter Three

Melanie

Another Friday, another night at The Mad House. Only this time, Tyler is here. We've been dating for three years. About two years too long. Deep down in my heart, I know I need to leave and break things off with him. But there's this stupid part of me that reminds myself of how much of my time I've already given him. Three years seems like a lot, even at twenty-five.

Breaking up would mean starting over. Going through the dating experience again. Dealing with whatever rumors may start in this small-town life. The trial-and-error process of dating until I find someone to stick with sounds so unappealing. I suppose I am content. That has to count for something, right?

We have good times. I just can't remember when the last one was. There's no light at the end of the tunnel to show when the next time might be.

In the beginning, Tyler was everything I thought I wanted and needed in a man. He was a gentleman. He was considerate and thoughtful. He remembered my birthday and gave me presents during the holidays. He was reliable.

At some point, things changed. He drank more and was angry often. He wouldn't come over, so I would always have to visit him. He stopped planning dates. We didn't go out unless it turned into a big argument, and he took me only after feeling guilty about it. I don't know what happened to him or why I haven't walked away yet. Something is better than nothing, right?

"Hey, Melanie." I turn to find Donna, whom we transported to the hospital a few weeks back. "Those blondies you gave me were delicious. Thanks again for making them."

My cheeks flame a little. I have a habit of baking sweets for random folks I interact with around Cardinal Point, and particularly if they are nice to me. Sometimes, it's patients we transfer, though. It's kind of hard not to do something thoughtful for them, especially if they had an ordeal. Thankfully, the town finds it endearing instead of weird.

I speak to Donna for a few minutes, promising to send over my recipe, before she steps away. I've turned back toward Tyler when somebody speaks.

"Wow, here last week with Austin and now here with someone else. You sure get around."

I tense at the sound of Angela's voice. Tyler, who was talking to one of his friends, stops and slowly pivots to look at me with a face of stone. That expression does not mean good things.

"Oops." She giggles and walks away.

"Who the fuck is Austin?" His buddies, cowards that they are, move off to play pool as Tyler's tone turns hard and angry.

"I didn't go out with him; I was here with his sister," I hurry to answer. Tyler isn't really the jealous type, but he has a fuse on him when he's been drinking, and Angela just lit it.

"It doesn't sound like you were with his sister. Who the fuck is he? You said nothing about coming here last week." He grabs my arm and yanks me towards him as he leans in until he's only a breath away. "You fucking around on me, Mel?" His voice is low and deadly.

"No!" How dare he accuse me of that? "Let me go." I attempt to yank out of his grasp, but it's useless. He only tightens his hold. "You're hurting me."

He pulls me closer, causing a yelp to leave me as he somehow squeezes my arm even harder. Before he can speak, I hear the worst possible voice I could hear right now.

"Everything okay, Melanie?"

Tyler raises a brow at me and then looks over at Austin. "You're interrupting us."

Austin ignores Tyler. "Melanie?"

"This him?" Tyler's tone is low and deadly. I whimper as his grip gets impossibly tighter.

"Let her go." Austin takes a step closer with his demand, just as Amelia bounces over.

"Melanie! I'm so happy to see you again. This must be the famous boyfriend."

I sigh in relief as Tyler finally releases me and turns his charming smile to Amelia, who introduces herself and mentions how I came here last week to hang out with her. God bless her.

Fury still vibrates off Austin, but Tyler acts oblivious. I rub my arm absentmindedly and then down the rest of my drink. Austin stalks off. Tyler returns to his friends after giving me a hard kiss.

"Girl," Amelia says in a low voice when he leaves. "You are in a mess. Come on." She loops her arm through mine, calls out to Tyler that she's stealing me away, and leads me over to their table. "Are you okay?" she asks as we take our seats.

"Fine." My hands tremble, though. Tyler has gotten violent with me before but never hinted at it in public. He's devolving further, I guess.

A drink appears in front of me, sloshing out of the sides as Austin sets it on the table a bit too hard. He glares at me, absolutely pissed. I ignore him and angle toward Amelia. The last thing I need is for Tyler to think I'm hanging out with Austin instead. Austin must realize this too. He moves to the other side of Amelia to talk to Silas.

"Do you want to talk about it?" Amelia asks. "Do you need help at all?" she adds softly.

Embarrassment washes over me. They believe I'm in an abusive relationship. I'm not.

Right?

A few hands-on arguments here and there is nothing to share. It really only happens when he's been drinking too much.

"I'm fine," I repeat, finally answering Amelia. "How are you?"

Amelia glances up at her brother, but I keep my gaze on her. She looks back at me with a smile. Amelia, my lovely new bestie, launches into telling me about her week. She seems like she loves to date and isn't shy about being forward with men. Only thirty minutes pass before Tyler stumbles over.

"Let's go." He pulls on my arm before I can stand.

All four guys at the table bolt to their feet as Tyler manhandles me.

"See you later, Amelia," I mumble.

"Are you sure you want to leave?" one guy asks. "Amelia can take you home later."

I don't have time to answer before Tyler drags me away. Austin takes a step toward us, but I shake my head. I'll be fine. There's no need for him to get involved. He'd only make things worse.

On the drive home, the car is quiet. Completely silent.

"You're fucking him, aren't you?" Tyler throws his accusation at me the moment he storms into the house with me following behind him.

"What? No!"

"Who is he, Mel?" he shouts, turning to face me.

"No one! His sister and I are friends. I hardly know him!"

"Don't lie to me." He closes the distance between us and grabs me by the throat. Terror sweeps over me. Tyler has never been like this. Never this angry. Never jealous. "I know you came to the bar with him and left with him."

"He gave me a ride," I wheeze.

Tyler knocks me against the wall. "How do you know him?" When I don't answer, his grip tightens. "What kind of fool do you take me for?" he yells.

Fury at his accusation causes me to erupt. "Fuck you!" How dare he accuse me of sleeping around when I've never even thought about fucking someone else. Sure, I've looked, but I didn't honestly entertain the idea *ever*. "You're an asshole, and if I were cheating on you, you'd deserve it!"

Tyler swings his fist, hitting my jaw so hard I fall onto my ass as black dots swim in my vision.

"You're a fucking whore." He spits, narrowly missing me, and storms into the kitchen.

Someone bangs on my front door.

With a wobbly balance, I stand and swing open the door. My eyes widen when I see Austin.

"You can't be here!" I whisper. "Go!"

I attempt to shut the door, but he reaches out and slaps his hand flat against the wood.

"He. Hit. You." Although he's not angry with me, I grip the handle tighter from the rage in his tone.

"Who the fuck is it?" Tyler shouts.

"Austin, *please* go." I hold my breath until his hand drops and he takes a step backward. Thankfully, he sees my desperation. "No one," I call back to Tyler. "Must be some kids." I close the door and turn to see Tyler disappear up the stairs with a bottle of liquor.

Thank goodness. He'll head to my room and drink himself to sleep. I plop onto my couch. My jaw throbs. After about thirty minutes and feeling fairly confident that Tyler is out like a light, I make myself a drink and head out to my front porch.

It's cool, quiet, and lovely. I sit on my swing, my mind spinning. What the fuck am I going to do? Tyler is dwindling fast. It's time. Time to think of an exit plan that will allow me to get out of this relationship unscathed.

"Can I join you?"

Austin stands before me. I didn't even hear him walk over.

"Want a beer?"

"No. You okay?" He sits next to me.

His body heat immediately envelopes me. It takes all I have not to lean into him. When I look at him, he steals my breath with how hard his features are. He's mostly cloaked in darkness with only my Halloween lights illuminating his face.

The streetlamp shows mine, though. Austin slowly lifts his hand and gently touches my jaw, causing me to flinch.

"I'm fine," I force myself to say.

"How long have you been with him?"

"Three years."

"How long—"

"Two, but the past six months have been an entirely different beast. I'm sorry about earlier, but he was accusing me of cheating on him with you and trying to find out how I knew you. If he realized you were here..." I shake my head.

"Why not say I'm your neighbor?" Austin's voice is carefully devoid of inflection.

I raise my eyebrows, surprised he would want me to share such a thing. "And have him still think I'm cheating? What if he confronts you and Erin is home? I couldn't do that to her. Besides, we're breaking up soon."

Austin seems to soften before my eyes. "Why have you stayed, if you don't mind my asking?"

I gulp down my drink. I need another one to get through that conversation. Without a word, I stand, walk inside to make another cocktail, and return with a beer in hand for Austin as well. He takes it and waits.

"It's stupid," I admit softly.

"Try me," he replies just as quietly.

With a sigh, I figure, what the hell? "I've already given him three years. He isn't always like this. I used to think he was perfect." I snort at that thought. "But I don't know. Any time I think about breaking up with him, I remember I'll be forced to date again. I'll have to find somebody all over *again*. What if I never find someone?" I stare into my drink as if it holds the answers.

"What if I'm fifty and never have kids? What if he's the best I can do? How many losers will I date before I find someone decent? It sounds like so much work. What if they are *worse* than he is? He's the devil I know. I just—"

"You're kidding me, right?" Austin interrupts. He sounds like he's in such a state of disbelief, I can't help but lift my head to look at him. "You're concerned you won't find someone else? Someone better?" He laughs. "Melanie, I promise, you'd find someone else and could be insanely happy in less than six months if you dumped him."

I bite my lip and then take a big swallow of my drink. I know I'm being silly, but it's worried me enough that I've stayed thus far. For Austin, who doesn't even know me, to think I'll find someone else in no time at all causes a warmth to rush through me.

"What if he refuses to go?" I whisper. Tyler frightens me more than he ever has now after tonight. He's never been like that with me. Not in public. Not over the idea of my cheating on him. I worry about how he'd react, even sober.

"You can call the law to escort him off your property. What's your number?" His phone is suddenly in his hand. I give him what he asked for without thinking. "I'll text you. If anything too crazy happens, you call me after you've called the cops."

There's no way I'm getting him involved, but I keep that to myself.

"You going to be okay here tonight?"

I nod and finish my drink. "He'll sleep until morning."

"I feel bad that I didn't know you had a boyfriend, especially a shitty one."

I shrug and yawn. Exhaustion settles over me like a blanket. My eyelids fight to stay open. "Thanks for checking on me," I mumble as I rest my head on his shoulder. "I'll break up with him tomorrow after work. But I'm not calling you if it goes sideways; you might be with Erin."

"Let me worry about Erin."

This is nice. It's been a long time since I could lean on someone else without them thinking it was because I was too weak to stand on my own. At least, I hope that's what he thinks. And Austin smells so good.

That's the last thing I recall before my alarm blares to wake me up for work. I rouse on the couch, wondering if Austin carried me or if I just don't remember walking inside.

It doesn't matter anyway. I get up and prepare for my day. Being a paramedic is not bad work, though it took me a bit to get used to my shift schedule. It's not my dream job either, but it pays the bills. All through the day, I wonder how my breakup conversation will go with Tyler.

It's time. I had to use way too much makeup to cover up what he did to me last night. I'd rather be alone for the rest of my life than be with someone like that. Besides, I've got Izzy, an old friend from high school, and now Amelia as friends. That's plenty.

Amelia has texted me periodically today, asking if I'm okay after last night. She wants details. She actually wishes to come over tonight, but I've got a hangover the size of Jupiter, and after work, I plan on crashing. Tyler may have to wait.

When I get home, my front door is ajar. I take slow, cautious steps as I approach the door, peek in, and gasp. The TV is gone, and some things are on the floor. The couch cushions look as if someone slashed them. All my Halloween decorations are out of place.

I glance over at Austin's place, but his truck isn't in the

driveway. After a moment, I run to lock myself inside my car and call the cops.

Forty-five minutes later, they confirm my house was broken into. My valuables stolen. My furniture was destroyed. It looks like I threw a wild party and let people trash my home. I try calling Tyler, hoping I can crash at his place tonight, but he doesn't answer. Fucking asshole.

"Melanie!"

I turn as Austin rushes inside.

"Are you okay?" he asks.

"Yeah. Someone broke in, stole some of my stuff, and ruined my things." I shrug, but my insides are shaking. All I wanted to do was come home and go to sleep. Now? I don't even want to stand here.

"Did you do it?" Austin asks when the last officer walks out of my house.

I am taken aback by his question. How can he ask me that? "I didn't do this!"

He shakes his head. "I meant breaking up with Tyler."

"Oh." My anger leaves me completely. "No. He won't answer my calls." I wrap my arms around myself in a hug. "I probably won't do it today," I admit. "I don't want to stay here, and I can crash at his place."

This is when it would be nice if my best friend, Izzy, had moved back home already. I could suck it up and stay with my dad or one of my brothers, but I really don't want to deal with their reaction when they find out about this.

"No, you aren't, but you can pack a bag." When my eyes widen, he says, "Amelia is at my house with Erin. You can crash at her place tonight. Go. I'll wait here." My mouth opens, and as if he knows I'm about to argue, he adds, "This is an out for you, Melanie. Take it."

He's right. I should start my path away from Tyler now. I nod and then pack a bag, hoping Amelia is okay with her brother offering me to stay with her tonight.

Chapter Four

Austin

"Everything okay?" Amelia asks the moment I walk into the kitchen with Melanie trailing behind me.

"Yeah. Melanie's sleeping over with you tonight."

"I don't have—" Melanie stops when I glare with a raised eyebrow at her.

"Sounds exciting," Amelia says. I'm not surprised she's rolling with this. Amelia has no problem with spontaneity. She doesn't need to know everything. She goes with the flow more often than not.

"Who are you?" Erin perks up. "Are you having dinner with us?"

"Yes," I answer before Melanie can wiggle out of it like she seems to want to do. "Baby girl, this is our neighbor, Melanie. Mel, this is my daughter, Erin."

The sweetest smile lifts Melanie's lips. "Nice to meet you, Erin."

I order everyone to sit while I grab paper plates for the pizza we picked up on the way back from our day of fun.

Erin talks a mile a minute about our time together to Melanie.

"Are you staying to decorate cookies with us? We're decorating Halloween creatures!"

"Let's save that for later, baby girl. Melanie and Aunt Amelia need to get home and rest. They can come back and help with the cookies tomorrow."

Erin gives me a small pout, but considering the night Melanie had last night and her day today, there's no reason to subject her to decorating cookies with a bouncy little girl. Just as Erin opens her mouth to argue with me, Melanie's phone rings. She glances at the screen and then at me.

"I should take this."

I watch as she stands and walks out the front door, answering the call.

"Daddy, I'm full. Can I play now?"

My gaze slides over to my daughter. "You only ate half a slice," I point out, causing her to shrug. "Go ahead."

She scrambles out of her seat and runs to her room. I swear she knows only one speed. I wasn't even supposed to have her this weekend, not that I'm complaining at all, but I'm suspicious of Angela since she's voluntarily giving me more time with Erin.

"So." Amelia grins. "You and Melanie."

I frown. "There is no me *and* Melanie. Her boyfriend is a piece of shit, and we both know part of the reason she had to deal with him last night was because of Angela. Someone broke into her house today; that's why the cops were over there. I can't have her stay with me since Erin is here, so she's staying with you. Don't get any wild ideas."

Amelia raises her eyebrows. "But you would let her stay here?"

I roll my eyes as Melanie walks back in. "Everything okay?"

"Yeah, it's done. Amelia, I'm gonna run. Just text me your address when you're home?"

Amelia stands. "No, we could go now, and you can follow me."

"He gonna cause trouble?" I ask.

Melanie shakes her head, but I'm not sure she's being honest. I don't even know why I care. I am not looking for a woman. Definitely not this woman.

The problem is that if I must have a weakness, it would be a damsel in distress. Melanie is a damsel in distress if I ever met one. The thought of her not being here under my roof where I can keep an eye on her makes my skin crawl. It's taking everything I have not to tell her I'll sneak her in after Erin goes to bed.

I say nothing. Amelia runs out of the kitchen to tell Erin goodbye, and I watch Melanie shift her weight. Her gaze bounces around the room. The fact she's uneasy causes my fingers to twitch with the urge to pull her against me and hold her tight.

"You gonna be okay?" I hate that I care about the answer.

Melanie nods. Amelia walks back into the room, gives me a quick hug, and then hooks an arm through Melanie's. She promises they'll return tomorrow. I also hate that I'm looking forward to seeing her again.

AUSTIN 8:30 PM

She holding up okay?

AMELIA 8:31 PM

She's fine. Leave us alone.

AUSTIN 9:15 PM

Did she say what happened with Tyler?
Does she think he'll bother her still?

AMELIA 9:20 PM

For someone who doesn't care and
doesn't like her...SUPPOSEDLY...you sure
are acting as if you do. She's not talking
about Tyler. She's asking me about you.

AUSTIN 9:21 PM

What are you telling her?

My sister never answered me last night, and she ignored any additional texts I sent. When Amelia comes over around one, I narrow my eyes at her.

"What are you doing here?"

"Did you hit your head or something? We're baking cookies."

"I thought we were waiting for Melanie."

Amelia sits next to me on the couch. "She doesn't want to come after work. Sorry."

"What did you say to her?" I ask as if this is Amelia's fault. As if this is a bad thing. It should be the best news I've heard all day.

My sister looks over at me and raises an eyebrow. Before she has a chance to answer, Erin rushes in. Guess we're making cookies. This is for the best. I don't want a relationship, and Melanie annoys me too much as it is. But the fact that someone violated her safe haven bothers me all day long. Just because I don't like her doesn't mean I want that uneasy feeling from someone entering her space without permission to invade her home. No one deserves that.

These thoughts run rampant in my mind until I leave

Amelia in charge to handle an errand and make a phone call. I'm being a good neighbor.

That's all.

I repeat that to myself as I replace and install Melanie's front door as well as all her locks.

I scream it at myself as I have a security system installed.

This should help her feel safe enough to return home, I hope. It's tempting to clean up the mess, but I don't want to violate her space anymore than I already have. My phone rings, and I answer the call from my best friend.

"Done swearing off women?" Silas asks. "I hear you've been busy today."

"First of all, how the fuck do you know what I've been doing?" Silas has an uncanny ability to learn about everything. They might as well crown him king of gossip. Silas only chuckles, so I address what he said. "I do one nice thing for someone and you jump to that conclusion?"

He chuckles. "Replacing the door, locks, and installing a security system isn't one nice thing. Does she even know you're doing this?" I must remain quiet for too long because Silas laughs harder. "You're fucked, Austin."

"Shouldn't you be working?" I snap, glancing at my watch. Melanie should be home soon.

Silas sobers. "Not everyone is Angela, Austin. If you're interested in her, sweet. But don't put that baggage on her and don't carry it with you. Otherwise, you might as well leave her alone."

Her car pulls into her driveway, so I step outside. "I've gotta go."

She parks and gives me a nervous smile as I hang up.

"Everything okay?" she asks once she gets out of her car.

"Fine. Figured you would want to stay home tonight, so

I replaced your door and your locks. I also, ah, installed a security system. Hope it makes you feel safer. Come on, I'll show you."

Her eyes are wide, but she follows me. I hand over her new keys and then explain the security system.

"What do you want for all of this?" she asks softly. Is she unable to accept an act of kindness without repaying it? "This all costs money, Austin," she points out as if I don't know that. "How much do I owe you?"

"Nothing." She opens her mouth to object, so I tack on, "Lenny, the guy at the hardware store, heard what happened and he donated the door and the locks. The guy who installed the system is a buddy of mine, and he also didn't charge me anything." The part about Lenny is true, but I paid the cost of the equipment. Lenny was all too happy to help; apparently, he's done a favor for Melanie before as well, and she repaid him with his favorite baked goods—lemon bars.

It hits me that she may be irritated at me for overstepping or pushing that button again, so I hurry to add, "I know you could've done this all yourself. I wanted to take this part off your plate for my own sanity. I'm sorry if—"

Melanie closes the distance between us and throws her arms around my neck, bringing my words to a full stop.

"Thank you, Austin."

I slowly embrace and then release her before the intoxicating feeling becomes too much because, *good goddamn*, she feels perfect. "Think you'll be okay here tonight?"

She nods.

"Text if you need anything. I should get home."

"Thanks again."

I nod and then hurry back to my house. Spending time near her is dangerous. Amelia eyes me, but I ignore her and

focus on my daughter, who shows off the cookies they decorated. I send her off to take a shower, feeling a little guilty
for not being here with them today. Taking care of Erin is
my first—my only—priority.

"Don't do that," Amelia says.

"Do what?" I ask as I clean up the kitchen.

"Feel guilty. That was a nice thing you did for Melanie.
She needed that more than you know. You're no less of a
good father for helping Melanie, and you deserve to be
happy with someone, be it her or someone else."

I glance over my shoulder at my sister. "What do you
mean, she needed that?"

"Not my story to tell. I didn't dive into your past with
her, and I won't do the same with you about hers."

Leave it to my sister to have morals. But I say, "It doesn't
matter; I'm not interested." My sister snorts, and the door-
bell saves me from responding further. I glare as I pass her
instead. No good is on the other side of my door. "You're
early."

Angela shrugs. "We are having dinner with Caleb's
parents. Is she ready?"

If I could strangle her with my bare hands, I would. Just
to get rid of her and have Erin all to myself. I step aside to
let her in.

"She's in the shower." I leave Angela and walk down
the hall to Erin's bathroom. "Baby girl," I call through the
door. "Mom's here to pick you up. You almost done?"

There's a beat of silence and then, "No."

I chuckle. She likes showers now, but that doesn't mean
she won't waste time in there, playing in the water and
sticking various toys to the tile.

"Hurry on up then." I step into her room and find clean
clothes for her to wear. Once finished, I lay them out on her

bed, knowing she'll come in here to get dressed. It's tempting to stay in here to avoid Angela, but I can't abandon my sister like that.

"Do you know who he's dating?"

"I'm not dating anyone," I say as I enter the room.

Angela jumps, startled that I heard her. God, she's stupid. My sister wouldn't tell Angela a damn thing about my personal life. Why Angela even wants to know is beyond me. I know better than to assume it's because of Erin.

Not wanting to be in the same room as the single-handedly most vile woman on earth, I return to the kitchen to finish cleaning up. Both Erin and Amelia make a freaking mess when they bake.

My phone vibrates with a text, and I pull it from my pocket.

MELANIE

Favorite dessert?

AUSTIN

You don't need to bake me anything.

MELANIE

Please.

AUSTIN

Apple pie

MELANIE

Thank you.

I still don't understand why she thinks she needs to bake *me* something.

I hear the shower turn off and after another minute or so, head back down the hallway to check on Erin. She's dressed and sitting on her bed.

42

"Will you brush my hair, Daddy?"

"Sure thing, baby girl."

I take her seat, and she pulls over a small chair to sit in front of me. Erin is quiet, which is unusual for her. She's normally chattering nonstop.

"Everything okay?"

She shrugs. "Can I ask something?"

"What's up?"

Her voice softens. "How come I don't get to live with you?"

I clench my jaw, but keep my brush strokes gentle as ever. "Mom makes the rules." While not the smartest thing to say, I'm over Angela always having the upper hand when it comes to Erin.

"The rules are stupid."

It takes everything not to laugh. "Just remember you're always welcome over here. I'll never say no. Mom said you're going to your grandparents tonight."

Maybe a shift in subject will brighten her mood. While Caleb's not my favorite person—since he was the one Angela cheated on me with—his parents have been nothing but good to my daughter. As a matter of fact, Caleb's only saving grace is that he's good to my daughter, too.

"Oh good. I miss Daddy Caleb."

I frown, confused by what she said. "What do you mean?"

"He's been staying with Pop and Nana."

I want to ask more, but I'm not putting Erin in the middle of whatever is going on. It sounds like Caleb and Angela are having problems, though.

Before I can formulate what to say, Erin speaks again.

"Are you and Mom going to live together again now?"

My chest tightens. "No, baby girl. We're not. Your mom and I aren't going to be together like that again."

"Because you don't love each other anymore? Is that why Daddy Caleb left too?"

Christ. How do I answer that? I never loved Angela the way I should have a woman I thought I might marry. Looking back, there were quite a few red flags for both of us.

"I'm not sure why Daddy Caleb left. As far as your mom and me are concerned, sometimes grown-ups realize they're better off not being together," I say carefully. "It doesn't mean we don't all love you more than anything in the world."

Erin nods slowly. I don't want her leaving the house with this on her mind, so I pivot the conversation to wrap this up.

"Tell you what. I'll talk to Daddy Caleb. Maybe next weekend the three of us will do something, okay?"

It was weird at first to get used to the idea of my little girl calling someone else daddy, but Caleb has been there for her since day one, and he doesn't do for her any less than I do. Angela insisted on it, probably hoping it would piss me off, but that backfired on her. He ended up being an unlikely ally when it comes to Erin; we both always have her best interests at heart.

The idea thrills Erin, and I quickly say goodbye to both my daughter and sister. For the next few hours, I eat, clean up the house, do laundry, and relax. My mind drifts, wondering how Melanie is doing. If the new security system and locks are actually making her feel safer.

Melanie isn't my problem, though. With a sigh, I amble into the kitchen for a glass of water, intent on going to bed, when I notice movement on Melanie's porch. As I squint, I realize it's her porch swing. Is she outside?

Before I can think better of it, I walk out my front door and across the yard to Melanie's.

"Hey," I say when I see her rocking slowly in the swing. "You okay?"

There's a water bottle in her hands, which she turns around and around.

"Hey, Austin," she replies without looking up.

I close the distance between us. My brows raise when I spot a handgun imprinting on her shirt by her hip. As I take a seat next to her, Melanie stands.

"Be right back." She slips inside, returning a moment later with another water bottle, handing it to me.

"You didn't have to do that."

She shrugs.

"What's wrong?"

Melanie sighs and looks over at me. "I appreciate what you did, I really do, but—"

"Not quite enough?" I bump my elbow against her hip and hit the butt of the gun, raising my eyebrows at her.

"No. I keep expecting someone to jump out at me or something." She waves a hand in the air. "I'll be fine. It's either get over it or move, and I don't want to move. Although that would be just as easy at this point since I have to clean that mess up and buy new furniture. I've spent all evening cleaning and only have my room and bathroom done."

"Aren't you supposed to be baking me a pie?"

She laughs as I hoped she would. "Tomorrow, I will; I have to go shopping first. Most of my bakeware was glass, and they broke all of it. Erin already headed back to her mom's?" she asks to change the subject.

"Yeah. Angela wouldn't let her take the Halloween cookies she made; if you want some, I can bring them over."

"Maybe," she agrees. "What do you do for work?"

"I make custom furniture and do reupholstery."

Melanie's eyes widen, and she smiles. There is definitely some black magic going on. I have a sudden, inexplicable need to see that smile more often; I'll be fucked if I were to witness it in the bright daylight instead of under these god awful Halloween lights.

"No way! Really? Do you own The Chair Necessities?"

I nod. "Yeah, that's me. We make custom pieces, do classes, and we've even been able to offer an apprenticeship program."

"Wow," she breathes. "It's so cool that you get to do something you love."

It's weird to watch her mood shift all because of my job and how interesting she finds it. She's had a rough few days, and I say, "If you want, you can stop by, and I'll show you the shop. Behind the scenes access." In reality, she won't be seeing anything anyone else can't see, but her excitement is clear immediately.

"Really? I would love that! Thank you."

We fall into a silence. It's oddly comfortable. There's the occasional sound of traffic somewhere in the distance, a dog barking here and there, and the consistent creak of her porch swing as we sway softly.

Still, after a few minutes, I break the quiet. It's late. She's had a long shift and has to be up early in the morning. I'm also doubting my sanity the longer I'm around her because all I want to do is pull her into my arms.

"You should get some sleep."

"I should."

We continue rocking gently back and forth on the porch swing. The temperature has dropped, and it's good and chilly now. I wish I had thought to snag a hoodie before walking over.

The cool air is all but forgotten when we stop swinging, and I notice Melanie peeling at the label of her bottle. She inhales deeply, as if needing to brace herself.

"Will you sit inside with me for just a little bit? Maybe that'll—"

Melanie stops talking when I stand and hold out my hand to her. She's nervous about being home alone, but doesn't want to leave. I can't say I blame her. She takes my hand, and I continue to be shocked at the urge to hold on tight and never let go. Who is this woman? What is wrong with me?

I manage to ignore the inner noise. We walk inside, sit next to one another on her new couch, and Melanie puts on *Little House on the Prairie*. I slouch down, resting my head on the back and stretching my legs out in front of me. My hands clasp on my stomach. It's been a long day. Maybe Melanie will doze off soon so I can get some sleep myself and forget all about her intoxicating presence.

Chapter Five

Melanie

I groan at the pain in my neck. God, stiff necks are the absolute worst. Maybe worse than a charlie horse cramp; at least those go away. Neck cricks are so painful, *and* they linger. As I pull my knees up, hoping to settle in for more sleep before my alarm goes off, I still as my senses become alert at the weight of hands on top of my legs and the feel of a presence beneath them.

What the hell?

Slightly afraid to open my eyes, I maneuver my leg until I pat the form with my foot. It's someone's lap. Oh, my God. Someone's on the couch with me!

"Feeling for something in particular?"

I shriek at the sound of a gruff, scratchy voice. I quickly tuck my legs to my chest and sit up. Last night clicks into place as I take in Austin, who's still next to me. We must've fallen asleep. My mouth parts to speak just as my alarm blares. Great. Time for work already. I hurry to turn it off and face my guest.

My voice catches in my throat with the look on Austin's face. He stares so intently at me. It's unnerving. I glance down at my shirt, wondering if I spilled something on it. There's nothing there. As I lift my head, Austin clears his throat and stands.

"I'm heading home. Have a good day."

"You too," I squeak.

My alarm sounds again, and I groan. Work is a distraction I need, anyway.

For two days, I work, replace my things, and bake to release the stress. I share the goodies with various folks I run into throughout my day. The town loves me if only because I share my baked goodies with them. There's no way I could eat everything all by myself.

On late Thursday afternoon, I go about delivering my baked goods specifically to those who helped fortify my home. I stop at the hardware store first to give Lenny his lemon bars.

"Oh, if it isn't my favorite child," Lenny booms the moment he sees me with a plastic container.

I giggle, as intended. "Mr. Lenny, you have four and none of them are me."

He walks around the counter to offer me a one-arm hug. "And yet, you're still my favorite. Are you sure I can't set you up with one of my sons? Then we can make it official."

I hand him his goodies. He cracks it open and doesn't waste any time taking a bite. He moans with much exaggeration, and I laugh again at his antics. "I'm officially single now, so I'll think about it."

He drops the bar back into the container and plops it on the desk. His hand clutches his chest. "Don't tease me, girl. I'll get all four of 'em in here in a heartbeat. I'd have to suggest my eldest, though he may be a bit old for you. He's got most of his wits."

My cheesy grin is unavoidable. "I'll see what I can do. I

just wanted to stop by and thank you for donating the material to Austin. I'm in your debt, so whenever you get a craving for sweets, let me know and they're yours."

Lenny dramatically leans on the long counter. "Melanie, my girl, you're going to give me a heart attack, offering unlimited sweets." He stands up and sheds his goofy demeanor, getting serious. "It was an honor to help; I'm sorry it happened, especially to such a sweet soul. If you need anything else, let me know." His eyes crinkle as if something occurs to him. "You're not with that Austin fella, are you?"

"Oh, no. He's just my neighbor; he's been looking out for me with everything going on."

"Good, good." Lenny nods. He slaps the counter. "I need to finish these." He picks up his goodies, and I take that as my chance to leave.

I bid him farewell and drive to my last stop: The Chair Necessities.

When I step into the storefront, which is located downtown, I'm awed immediately. The craftsmanship in the work is obvious. Be it a dining room table, a rocking chair, or an end table. It's all gorgeous.

"Excuse me, ma'am, but you can't bring food in here."

I whirl around at the sound of a woman's voice and spot narrowed eyes from the woman standing behind the counter.

"I'm, uh, actually here to see Austin."

Her mouth flattens more. "Do you have an appointment?"

"No, but—"

"Sorry. He's unavailable."

Her curtness annoys me, and I find myself saying, "He told me to swing by. Can you let him know I'm here?"

"He's not in."

What is this girl's problem? He is here because I texted him I was coming, and he said I was welcome to stop by. Oh God, is he seeing her? We enter a standoff with a staring contest as I debate what to do. I don't want to interfere somehow if he's seeing this woman, but I would like to thank him for what he's done.

With that thought, I pull my phone out and call him.

"Hey," he answers within three rings.

"Hey. I'm here, but your cashier says you're not. Do I need to come back?"

Austin sighs. "Sorry, she can take her duties a little too seriously. I'll be right up."

With restraint I didn't know I had, I ignore his employee and return my focus to the rocking chair, in particular. Within a minute, I hear a door and footsteps. I turn around and see Austin round the corner. His gaze drops to my hands.

"That my apple pie?" he asks with a small smile.

I glance over at his cashier. She's flat out glaring at me now. Focusing on Austin, I answer him. "Depends."

"On?"

"Do I get to see the back?"

Austin laughs and waves for me to follow him, his cashier glaring daggers at me the entire time. I watch in fascination as it disappears when Austin looks at her. "Stacey, this is Melanie. She's welcome anytime, okay?"

She beams a smile that a moment ago I would've sworn she wasn't capable of, and nods. "Of course."

Austin thanks her before pushing open the door, a hand finding the small of my back as he allows me to step in first. The space at the rear opens up like a warehouse. It's big and open. He takes the dessert and drops it in an office before leading me over to a workstation. A few other people are working, but they don't seem to notice us.

"I'm in the process of fixing this beauty up for her owner." The beauty in question is a wingback chair with green floral fabric that is falling apart so much that the stuffing pokes out of the cushions. "She was gonna throw her away, but there's no need when I can make her look brand new again." Austin picks up a beautiful blue fabric, which is what he will use to recover the chair.

Austin takes my hand and leads me near the workstation of someone else. I watch in amazement as the man works a piece of wood on a woodturner. The shape seems vague to me now, but after seeing that rocking chair, I can only imagine how beautiful it will be. Austin leads me to someone else who repairs an old wooden high chair. Most of these guys look to be the same ones I saw him with at The Mad House.

It's clear that this business is his passion. He talks in depth about the process, from the techniques to the woods to the fabrics. Who knew there was so much to know about furniture?

Austin glances at his watch, and I wonder if I've overstayed my welcome. Before I can mention leaving, though, he looks over at me.

"Got some more time? Was thinkin' about headin' to Go Ahead and Fry Me for supper."

His offer surprises me. Austin has been nice to me, but I figure it's because of my circumstances. Still, I nod. Supper sounds good, especially since I missed lunch. We ride together even though the diner is literally right up the road. We could've walked.

As we enter, Mrs. Edna, one of the owners, sees us and gushes so loudly that the entire town can probably hear her.

"Oh my. Millie!" she calls out to her best friend, who is currently in the kitchen. "Austin is here on a date with a woman!" She claps her hands excitedly while Austin tenses next to me. "And it's Melanie!" She finally closes the distance between us, and nearly every eye in the diner is on us.

Mrs. Edna and Mrs. Millie both act like anyone younger than them is a child or grandchild to them. It comes as no surprise when we both get a peck on the cheek and a hug, as do most regulars in our age group. That is, if the two old ladies know and like you. They treat most of the town as family, and that's another reason I love this place.

She grabs a pair of menus and leads us over to a nearby booth. "I'm so happy to see you two. Oh, you're so adorable. It was her baking that sucked you in, I bet."

"This is *not* a *date*," Austin snaps harshly. He makes a date sound like the most disgusting thing on the planet. Mrs. Edna loses her temporary bliss.

"Oh, I'm sorry." She clears her throat. "Do you two know what you want?"

"My usual, please," Austin replies.

Mrs. Edna turns to me, and I blurt out the first thing I spot on the menu. She steps away, leaving me with a stewing Austin. I'm uncertain if he's furious because she told everyone about his date, or because it's with *me*. The silence is uncomfortable. Part of me wants to break it, but at the same time, Austin completely ignores me. His gaze remains on his hands until the door opens and in walks someone who snags his attention.

Mrs. Edna quickly leads him to a spot at the bar, and Austin raps his knuckles on the table.

"I'll be right back. I need to talk to Caleb for a second."

With my nod, he hurries toward the bar away from me. Mrs. Edna returns to our table to drop off our drinks.

"Actually, Mrs. Edna, I have to run. Can you cancel my order? I'm so sorry for the inconvenience."

She glances between Austin at the bar and me, her eyebrows furrowing and her lips pulling down into a frown. "Are you sure you can't wait a few and I can get it to-go for you?"

I shake my head. Austin did everything in his power to ignore me after the misunderstanding; I have entirely too much to do to sit here and be ignored. I don't deserve the way he's treating me.

"I'm sure."

As I stand from the booth, she asks, "Does Austin know you're leaving?"

"Yes," I lie. "Sorry, gotta go."

And then I high-tail it out of there. Literally. The moment I quietly escape from the diner, I run all the way back to The Chair Necessities. Darkness cloaks the sky now, and my skin prickles as if someone's watching me. Once I'm in my car, I swing by a fast-food restaurant for dinner and drive home.

I'm not sure why Austin's reaction bothers me so much. Amelia hinted he'd been fucked over, and after meeting Angela, I'm not surprised. It was such a harsh response. It's hard not to take it personally. At home after I eat, I grab my headphones, turn the music up, and start cleaning.

Yes, my house is finally clean after what happened, but it feels as if an unwelcome filth remains. It's like whoever broke in is still here. My music pauses with a text. I decide to pay no attention to it in case it's Austin. Instead, with my bucket of soapy water and a brush, I kneel on the kitchen tile and scrub. Maybe the harder I clean, the more exhausted I'll get, and the easier it'll be to ignore how unsettled I still feel.

It's not like I can ask Austin over every night. And I don't want to move. I sigh and wipe my forehead with the back of my hand. There has to be a solution. Maybe I'll magically get over it in the next half hour? One can hope.

The music pauses to indicate an incoming call. That brief pause is enough for me to hear pounding on my front door. I pull out my earbuds. Yeah, someone is definitely here. What the hell?

"Melanie! Open the fucking door before I break it down!"

Austin? The urgency in his voice has me standing and running over to fling my door open. Seeing a slightly unhinged Austin widens my eyes, but my gaze is pulled to the orange blaze behind him.

"Are you okay?" he asks as I blurt, "Shit! My yard is on fire!"

Sirens wail in the distance. When I try to push past Austin, he stops me.

"Are you okay?" he repeats.

"Yeah. I was cleaning."

"You've pissed someone the hell off, Mel." When I frown, he tilts his head toward my door.

I look over and gasp. Someone painted in bright red paint one word on my brand new, beautiful white door.

SLUT

"I came home and saw the fire. Looks like someone tore down all your decorations and made a bonfire. You didn't hear anything?"

The skepticism written all over his face pisses me off.

"You think I did this?"

His features relax and soften. "No. It's just...somebody was brazen enough to do this while you were home, Melanie."

What he says sinks in as the fire department parks along the curb and begins extinguishing the blaze. Vaguely, I hear Austin ask for my phone to check the cameras I forgot I had. My eyes remain glued to the flames and the firefighters.

Someone yanked down all my Halloween decorations, put them in a pile around my gorgeous tree, and then lit them on fire. They must've doused it in an accelerant because the fire is really going. Then they painted a nasty word on my door.

I was at home the entire time.

Arms wrap around me, and I'm being walked back inside. I sit when pushed to sit. I hand over my phone. I answer the questions thrown at me. It seems they snuck up, careful of the cameras, and then spray painted them to make their job easier. I don't understand who would do this.

My phone rings, and Austin hands it over to me.

Izzy.

With a sigh, I answer.

"Mel! Why haven't you called me? Someone broke into your house over a week ago, and you didn't call!"

"I'm sorry. Look, can we connect another time? Someone just painted slut on my door and set all my decorations on fire."

Izzy yelps. She's quiet for all of a second before she asks, "Do you want me to come back? Be an extra body in your house so you aren't alone?"

I squeeze my eyes closed. There's nothing I'd love more.

Izzy left Cardinal Point right after high school to work on a cruise line and recently resigned in order to travel across the States. It's all a way to avoid moving back and potentially facing the years-long pen pal she's in love with. The fact that she's offering to come back for me is huge.

At the same time, I don't want to be the reason she returns after all these years. Even if I don't think I'll ever sleep again.

"No, don't come home on my account; I'll be okay. I'll stick it out and figure something out."

"Is that even safe?"

Probably not, but... "I'll be fine. Call you tomorrow, alright?"

Izzy says something before hanging up, but I'm already spacing out. Austin sits next to me until all the first responders leave. Silence falls over us. Austin grabs my hand so gently within his.

"Are you okay?" he asks softly.

I shake my head. His arms wrap around me, but all I feel is numbness.

"Do you want me to stay, or would you like to come to my house?"

"You don't have to stay," I answer.

"That's not what I asked."

Why is he even *here*? Why is he trying to comfort me? This is the same man who couldn't tolerate the idea of people thinking we were on a date.

At that thought, I pull away and stand.

"I don't need your help. Lock the door on your way out."

I escape to my room and plop onto the bed once I've changed and brushed my teeth. Normally, I sleep without a TV, but not since this nonsense started. I hear every little sound, and I'd rather not. My imagination runs wild regardless.

For what feels like forever, I toss and turn until I fall asleep. But in my dreams, I'm haunted.

No, not haunted.

Hunted.

Some monster chases me around my house, always on my heels.

My heart pounds hard in my chest. Hard enough that I worry my body will give out on me.

My breath labors until I'm on the verge of hyperventilating.

Suddenly, I find myself in a windowless room.

I twirl around and around and around, hoping to discover an exit when there clearly isn't one.

Until a door appears on one wall, but there's no knob. I slap an open palm repeatedly against the wood.

My mouth opens to yell, but no sound comes out.

Smoke filters through all the cracks.

Oh my God. Are they burning me alive?

Putrid black smoke fills the room, suffocating me. Like in some horror movie, a beam mysteriously falls from the ceiling all ablaze. I whirl around and scream bloody murder as a dark,shadowy figure appears out of nowhere.

"Melanie! Melanie! *Mel!*"

With a shriek, I awaken and scream again at the form hovering over me.

"Mel, it's just me. It's Austin."

He pulls me upright and into his arms while simultaneously reaching over to turn on my lamp. I relax a bit at seeing him, but then I tense.

He's in my house. I kicked him out who knows how long ago.

"W-w-what are you doing here?" Fear still grips my heart like a vise.

If it's possible for this gorgeous man to look embarrassed, he does. "I never left," he admits. "Couldn't manage to leave, just in case. I was out in the hallway when I heard you thrashing and whimpering."

"You were in the hallway?"

He nods. "On guard duty."

Oh my. I'm not emotionally capable of handling what that does to me. My stomach flips and wreaks havoc that isn't all that terrifying. It's actually nice?

I don't understand what this is with Austin.

Not at all.

Chapter Six

Austin

"That's the nicest thing anyone has ever done for me," Melanie whispers.

I give her a small smile. "Any time. You okay?"

She shrugs.

Remembering everything that happened today, I clear my throat, untangle myself from her, and stand. "I'll be outside if you need anything."

I barely move an inch before she has a death grip on my wrist.

"Will you stay? In here, I mean?"

Like I could tell her no. I walk around and climb onto her bed with my back against the headboard. Melanie tugs on my arm until I'm lying next to her.

"Can I ask you something?" When she nods, I add, "Why did you run out on me at the diner?"

She throws an incredulous look my way. "Seriously? You acted like it was such a horrible, disgusting idea for people to think you were on a date with me."

I breathe out softly. "It wasn't that." She raises an eyebrow at me in disbelief. "It wasn't so much you as the date part." I sigh and focus back on the ceiling. "Angela was a major bitch who cheated on me while I was in the service, and she was pregnant with Erin. Every woman after her—the few that there were—has either been just as dishonest or Angela threatens to take me to court because somehow these women are a threat to Erin.

"I got tired of dealing with all of that and swore off women. So, no, I didn't like the idea of someone believing I was on a date when I don't date, and the last thing you need is Angela thinking there's something going on. I have no clue why she cares, but I don't trust her right now. She's lying to me about things with Erin and—" I cut myself off and shake my head. I don't need to bare my soul to my neighbor.

"I get it," she says, though she doesn't. There's no way for her to understand fully, but I appreciate the sentiment anyway. "Thank you for explaining. And for staying."

I reach over, grab her hand, and squeeze before releasing it and resting both of mine on my stomach. I want to ask her if she's sure she doesn't know who may do these things to her, but she needs rest.

"Get some sleep. You're safe."

She exhales softly and then rolls onto her side, facing away from me. Now that I'm lying down as well, exhaustion coats me. It's not like I was getting any shut-eye camped outside of her room. Within minutes, my eyes close.

I am situated between the cradle of a woman's hips, held up by my arms, as I rock into her. God, she feels fucking amazing. My gaze lifts from where our bodies meet, traveling slowly over her stomach, gorgeous tits, and then lands on her face.

Melanie's mouth parts in a perfect circle as she moans. My hips thrust into her again. Her nails dig into my shoulders, and she clenches around me.

"Fuck, Mel," I rumble.

As my hips thrust once more, I pause. My voice sounded entirely too loud and...real. My dick throbs, and my lower body presses forward again involuntarily. I withhold a groan at the feel of a delicious ass.

Reality trickles in a bit more. My eyes pop open, and I freeze. Melanie is exactly as I remember seeing her last. However, I am cuddling with her. My arm drapes over her waist, my face presses into the hair gathered at her neck, and my body fits tight against her.

Fuck.

She's too still in my arms, which means she's pretending to be asleep while I freaking assault her. I also pretend she's asleep and what just happened didn't as I carefully extract myself from her. Before I can fully climb out of bed, there's a loud banging on the door.

Melanie startles and sits up immediately.

"Expecting someone?"

She glances over at me, her cheeks turning pink. God, she's fucking cute; just strike me down now. "No."

When Melanie doesn't get up, I do and say, "C'mon. Let's see who it is."

We leave her room, and Melanie must feel a bit more at ease because she hurries toward the entrance and peeks through the peephole. Her body relaxes. A moment later, she throws open the door.

"Daddy!"

An older gentleman rushes her, quickly wrapping her in a hug.

"Melanie Rose, how is it that I had to hear at the general store this morning that someone broke into and vandalized your home?" He looks her over before pulling her into another embrace, which is when he notices me. "And who is this?"

"That's my neighbor, Austin. Sorry, I didn't call, but—"

"It doesn't matter now. Go pack a bag; you're staying with me."

"But there's no—"

"Nonsense," her father interjects. "You aren't safe, so you will stay with me where I can watch over you until we find this lunatic."

For the next five minutes, I observe as Melanie tries her hardest to explain that she doesn't want to stay with him and how he interrupts her each time, insisting he needs to look after her. With every objection, her shoulders fall until she's overcome with defeat.

As her dad makes another attempt to pull her away, Melanie catches my gaze. She gives me a small smile. "Thanks, Austin."

"Anytime. Catch you later."

I haul ass out of there, wondering if her father smothering her is why she feels the need to be independent. I spend all day thinking about Melanie, and I wonder if she will have to stay at her dad's place until they catch the person harassing her.

Work is busier than usual, which I appreciate. Restoring furniture fulfills me in ways I never expected. We take something broken, worn, almost forgotten—and make it beautiful again.

I run my hand over the arm of the chair I'm working on. It's a Victorian piece, over a hundred years old. The previous owner found it in her grandmother's attic, covered in dust and mouse droppings. The fabric was shredded, the stuffing spilling out, the wood scratched and dull.

Most people would have thrown it away. She brought it to me instead.

I've spent the last few weeks on this chair. First, I stripped the old finish and then worked the wood until the grain emerged, rich and warm. Now I'm ready for the final step—applying the new fabric, bringing the piece back to life.

Most people don't think twice about what we do. The joy, for me at least, is in how every piece tells a story. Maybe of the life it lived, the love the family had for it, and the life it can have again with future generations. People come and go, but there are certain things in life that find themselves passed down and becoming heirlooms. To have a hand in adding to its longevity, it's an honor.

That's what I love about the work I do. It helps that today it's distracting me from a certain woman I can't stop thinking about. The work keeps my mind off checking my phone every five minutes like some lovesick teenager. As if she has a reason to reach out.

Later, I'm in my office, doing a little paperwork after

ordering lunch for my guys, when Stacey pops in with the mail.

"Good weekend?" she asks.

"Yep. You?"

"Could've been better, honestly." She pauses, as if hoping I'll probe instead of studiously opening and checking what's inside the envelopes she handed me. "Do you think you'll ever get married?"

Her question is out of left field; still, I snort immediately at the idea of marriage. "Absolutely not." An unbidden image of the Melanie in my dream appears in my head just then. I shake my head to shoo it away. I'm sex-deprived; that's the only reason she's even on my mind.

Stacey's voice softens, and the air thickens as I realize what she just asked me. "Such a shame. Everyone needs someone to take care of them. Who really sees them."

I keep my gaze on the bill in my hands. "I'm good, Stacey. No need to worry."

There's a pause and then, "Good to know, but if you ever need anything, anything at all, I'm here."

I swallow hard. What am I supposed to say to that? Thanks, but no thanks? Please leave and remember you're my employee? Right or wrong, I decide to be an ass in hopes it nips whatever this is in the bud. "Just need someone back up front."

She mutters an *of course* and leaves my office.

I stare at the closed door for a long moment. Stacey's worked for me for years. She's always been helpful, maybe a little too helpful, but I've never thought much of it. This conversation sits wrong in my gut, though. She's never made me pause with discomfort until today.

I shake it off. She's just being nice. That's all.

Once our pizzas from Pizza Heaven Pizzeria are delivered, I abandon my office to eat with the guys in the workshop. It's a habit we've kept since the early days—gathering around whatever flat surface is clean enough, sharing food, and shooting the shit like we used to in the barracks.

These men followed me here after we got out because of the bond forged during our time in the service. And many had no clue what the hell we were supposed to do when we got our discharge papers. The idea of sticking together and working together was appealing, that they took me up on the offer, though Dean and Silas both work at the police department. There are days like today when they manage to swing by and grab a bite, if they can.

"You're quiet today, Lowe," Matthew Lankford observes. The habit of calling one another by our last names is still one we haven't fully broken. "Everything okay?"

"Fine. Just thinking."

"About that neighbor of yours?" Dean waggles his eyebrows.

"Mind your business."

"That's a yes," Silas translates. "He seems distracted to me. The kind that is because of a woman."

"I'm not distracted."

Everyone laughs, clearly not believing me, except for Stacey, who has been quiet. I flip them off, but there's no heat in it.

"Seriously though," Dean says, sobering slightly. "It's good to see you interested in someone. Been a long time."

"Too long," Silas agrees. "We were starting to worry you'd die alone with seventeen cats."

"I'm not interested in her." A little voice whispers, *Liar.* "And I don't like cats."

"Exactly. That's how bad it was going to get."

I shake my head, but I'm smiling. These idiots drove me crazy during our enlistment, and they drive me crazy now, but I wouldn't trade them for anything. When Angela was making my life hell, they had my back. When I was drowning in the early days of the business, they worked overtime without complaint.

Building this business from nothing was only possible because these men believed in me when I barely believed in myself. The military taught us to work as a unit, to trust each other with our lives. That doesn't just disappear when you trade camo for civilian clothes.

"Alright, lunch is over." I stand and stretch. "Back to work. We've got orders to fill."

"Sir, yes, sir," Matthew drawls, and barely dodges the shop rag I throw at his head.

On the way home, I talk to Erin on the phone, who is staying with her grandparents this weekend, and then eat dinner while watching TV. The fall air feels amazing today, so I step out onto my back porch to lounge and enjoy the weather.

Before I can sit, I hear music playing from next door. Melanie's home? I walk until I peer over the fence before I second-guess myself. She sits on her patio with a plate of pie in her hands. Leaving my own yard, I lift her gate lock and push the door open.

She lifts her head and gives me a small smile. "Just waltzing into my backyard now? You really don't have an understanding of boundaries, do you?"

"Only because you have pie and maybe a tiny part of me wanted to check on you. I thought you'd be at your dad's." I take a seat in the rocking chair opposite her.

"I snuck away earlier and told him I was staying with a friend. Want some then? It's sweet potato."

"Sure." As if I'd ever turn down food when she's the one offering.

She places her plate on the small table between us and disappears inside, returning within a minute with another slice of pie and a bottle of water, which she hands to me.

"Thanks. Will you be okay here tonight?" I bring a bite to my mouth and nearly groan. I didn't realize sweet potato pie could taste this damn good.

"Yeah, I think so. They replaced the cameras. Amelia offered to come over, too." It doesn't surprise me that my sister made the same offer. "I just…I don't know who would do this. I thought maybe Tyler, but he stopped by earlier—"

"He what?" Fury immediately rages within me. The last time she was around him, he left her with a bruise. He hurt her. Why would she let him within spitting distance of her? In fact, this town is too small for him to be in it with her.

"He was picking up some of his things and bragging that he's already moved on, apparently. I feel like someone is attacking the wrong person." She stabs at her dessert, and before I can respond, she changes the subject. "Did you enjoy the pie?"

I glance down at my empty plate. "Best sweet potato pie I've ever had. You should be a baker."

The most gorgeous smile lifts her lips. "That used to be my dream."

"What changed?"

The expression fades. Melanie takes our plates inside and returns a moment later. She swiftly dives into a new topic again. We talk about lighthearted things, mostly. She asks me about my daughter, and I share easily. She tells me about how her parents divorced when she was a kid and she ended up staying with her father, which surprises me. How did he manage that?

Melanie doesn't speak much about her mom, though. She also mentions two brothers, both of whom read her the riot act together. If I had to guess, they all baby her and think she can't do anything on her own.

At some point, the air nips our exposed skin as darkness falls. Melanie invites me inside, but I hesitate. Spending time with her is easy. It's nice. It's totally not what I need and definitely not what she needs once Angela catches wind of it.

Yet I follow her anyway as if someone has stolen my choice to choose otherwise.

"What is that smell?" Whatever it is, it smells delicious.

"Bread. I've been working on a loaf."

God, the woman can bake, and it might be one of my favorite things about her. The timer goes off, and Melanie pulls the pan from the oven.

"I love warm bread so much. We'll give it a minute and then have a slice."

I watch in fascination as she leans forward and takes a hearty inhale of the fresh bread. Why the fuck is that so hot? Was my brain recently deprived of oxygen? That's the only logical conclusion.

"Austin?"

I blink and refocus to see Melanie holding a slice out to me. I take a bite and moan in appreciation. It's a sweet bread, and it's so fucking delicious.

"We're gonna have to get married," I blurt out.

Melanie laughs as if I'm joking. I'm not. In fact, I'm dead serious. Aside from my mom, I don't think I've ever met a woman who can cook as well as Melanie. Well, bake. I know women are supposed to be my enemy, but I could forget all about that if it means having full access to the goodies Melanie mixes up.

"That sayin' about the way to a man's heart is through his stomach is a sayin' for a reason. It's true. I'll buy a ring tomorrow. We could get married on Monday at the courthouse, I'm sure."

Melanie laughs again while I pluck another slice of bread. "Well, sucks for you. I find you too annoying."

I bring a hand up to my heart. "That hurts, Mel. Can you hate me and still bake for me, though? That matters the most."

She laughs once more, and I swallow hard as I watch her. She's beautiful; she really is. But that's not why I'm here. I don't want a relationship. My hands are full with my daughter and with dealing with my never-ending problem of an ex.

After I scarf down the slice of bread, I clear my throat. "I should head back." The tension that quickly spreads through Melanie makes me hesitate. "Want me to camp out on the couch? I don't mind staying over again."

Her cheeks flush pink. Why would they do that? Maybe she's embarrassed I've offered. Unless...God, is she thinking about this morning?

"I'll be okay," she replies softly. "Alerts pop up on my phone any time the cameras pick up movement now, so I'm as safe as I can be."

I nod in acceptance. "Text me if you need anything."

Everything in my gut tells me to stay, but I have no reason. I turn and head back to my house, wondering what the fuck is wrong with me that this woman has me in knots.

Around three in the morning, I wake up restless. After about ten minutes of tossing and turning, I get up for a glass of water. Like the stalker I'm becoming, I can't resist walking over to peer out my kitchen window. What the fuck? All the lights are on at Melanie's. Was she unable to sleep with them off or is she still awake?

Without using any better judgment, I send her a text.

AUSTIN

Mel, you up?

It takes only a minute before she replies.

MELANIE

Yes. Can't sleep.

AUSTIN

I'm coming over.

This is ridiculous. There's no need for her not to get some rest. I know she's frightened, but she slept well last night while I was there. I jog next door, and Melanie has the door open by the time I arrive. The exhaustion seems to weigh heavily on her frame.

"You don't have to be here," she says as I open her storm door and step inside.

I close the door and lock it. "You don't have to be alone," I argue back. "Come on."

I snag her hand and lead her to her room, turning off lights as we go. We settle into her bed much like we did last night. Melanie whispers a thank you, and within five minutes, her breathing steadies.

It's an empowering, heady, fucking feeling to know she can rest easy because she feels safe with *me*.

Who the fuck even cares? Why does pride swell in my

chest, knowing I'm the reason she's getting some rest? Melanie is fucking with my head more than I'd like to admit. We aren't even sleeping together,for God's sake.

I close my eyes and shut my mind down. I'll deal with this tomorrow.

Or maybe never if I'm lucky.

Chapter Seven

Melanie

Yesterday morning, I woke with Austin wrapped around me and then him thrusting his erection against my ass in his sleep. This morning? I might as well be glued to him.

His body heat wraps me in a cocoon, and somehow, he makes the perfect pillow. His arm bands around me as if he needs to keep me in place. I need to move, though. My alarm will probably go off any minute, and the last thing I need is for Austin to catch me like this with him, especially after yesterday.

Austin's hand slides from my waist to my ass. I hold my breath as he presses me impossibly closer to him and squeezes my ass. With how he annoys me, I didn't expect him to be this kind with an attractive personality. I'm torn on whether it's a good thing that he's been around so much lately.

I ease my leg that I had thrown over his hips down and freeze when I feel his erection. My God, even in his sleep the man is horny.

Austin hums, grabs the back of my thigh, and pulls until

I'm practically on top of him, his hard-on nestled between my legs. This is bad. I need to get up, but how?

My alarm blares loudly in the room. In an instant, Austin stills beneath me. Maybe if I don't move, I'll disappear into thin air.

"You gonna roll off me and turn that off?" Austin's sleepy voice rumbles.

When I take no action because I'm frozen with embarrassment, Austin rolls us both, nabs my cell, turns off my alarm, and rolls us back like we were.

After a moment, Austin grunts as his hips flex. "If you ain't gonna get up, Mel, we're gonna have to think about a friends with benefits relationship since you don't want to marry me. It feels entirely too fucking nice to have you pressed against me like this."

Friends with benefits? That doesn't sound half bad. I can get what's bound to be a good fuck without being tied down in another relationship already. Maybe it'll expel some of the weirdness hanging around Austin and me.

I lift my head. "Seriously?"

"You give me the green light, I'll have your clothes off in less than five seconds."

"I've never..." Okay, this is actually a stupid idea. I've never done friends with benefits. What if things become complicated?

Austin groans, and his hands cup my face. "You're grindin' into me, Mel." Shit. I am. "No strings. Easy peasy." Still, I hesitate. "I don't want a relationship." The stark honesty in his eyes surprises me. "Even if I did, we start somethin', I'd keep you hidden."

Ouch. That hurts.

His thumb brushes across my lips. "Not for any reason

other than you have a shit ton on your plate already and the last thing you need is to be on Angela's radar."

His tone drops. "You're fucking gorgeous, Melanie. Put me out of my misery and fuck me, will ya?"

"You're thinking with your dick."

He rolls us until he's on top of me. "I don't see your point." He watches me carefully as he leans down and presses a kiss to my lips. It's the lightest, softest touch. As if he's testing the waters, waiting to see if I'll bite or not.

"No strings?" I ask as if I need him to promise me.

One of his hands travels down my side as he nods. "No strings. Our secret."

Instead of overthinking it for a moment longer, I lift up and kiss him. That's all it takes for him to lose his reservation and deliciously attack my body. I sure as hell hope I won't regret this.

After a fast, very hot round between the sheets this morning, I get ready for work. By the time I exit the shower, Austin is gone. No strings really means no strings. Perfect. After the disaster of my relationship with Tyler, I'm not exactly eager to date someone.

When Amelia messages me that everyone is getting together at The Mad House and she wants me to come, I decide, why the hell not? That's how I find myself sitting next to her, surrounded by a bunch of men.

Other than a quick hello, Austin doesn't pay me any attention. It's a relief to see that he's sticking to our no strings attached agreement. It didn't occur to me how this might affect my newfound friendship with Amelia if she were to find out.

"You'll never believe who asked me out today," Amelia squeals with excitement. She's been bustling in her seat since I sat down as if she was trying to hold it in, and she's finally burst.

I flick my gaze to the rest of the table. Though it seems like Silas is frozen solid, nobody pays attention to us.

"Gregory Caldwell!"

I hum in agreement. Gregory is a police officer in Cardinal Point, and he's a solid guy. I don't think there's a woman in this town who wouldn't be excited if he asked them out.

"What do you know about him? All I know is he's fucking hot. I tried to ask Silas, but he wouldn't tell me anything." She sends a glare his way. It makes sense that she'd pepper him with questions. He's on the police department with Gregory. Amelia refocuses on me and squeals in excitement again. "Spill! I'm beside myself with how excited I am, and I need all the details."

A loud noise startles us, and we realize Silas slammed his beer down on the table. Amelia frowns before ushering me out of the seat and tugging me toward the bar.

"That was odd, right?"

My new friend sighs and shifts direction until we're in a corner, far away from eavesdroppers, though one look shows that Silas watched us go. Definitely weird.

"Can you keep a secret?"

My mind immediately goes to how I slept with her brother this morning. I don't plan to let that slip to anyone. I nod.

Amelia leans in and whispers in my ear. "Silas and I... are kind of...sleeping together." My eyes widen to the size of saucers at this. "Strictly friends with benefits. We both had a bit too much to drink one night, not drunk, but more than tipsy. Okay, so it was more me than him. Anyway, he saw to it I got home and well, when I launched myself at him, he didn't fight me off. We've been...hanging out...since."

"Are you sure it's just sex?" My gaze flicks back to him. While he's not watching us, he still seems tense. "He doesn't seem happy about your date."

Amelia rolls her eyes. "That's because he'd lose his fuck buddy, and our chemistry is off the charts." She fans herself with a grin before waving away the topic. "He'll be alright. He was very clear that nothin' would ever come of it, and I take his word at face value. We're just...there...when we need a release or maybe a friend. We hang out sometimes, but we're never gonna have a relationship, which is perfectly fine."

Amelia seems convinced of this. However, now I'm confused because it sounds as if they spend time together outside of sex. And Silas looked like he was trying too hard not to react to what Amelia said, which caused the biggest reaction.

"Are you sure Silas is on the same page?" I can't help but ask.

"Positive. Anyway, what do you know about Gregory? Being a local, I assume you have the dirt."

I shrug. "He's a good guy. Best friends with the chief, even though he's old enough to be his father. I've never heard anyone speak ill of him."

"And he's hot." She waggles her eyebrows.

I nod. That he is. I don't think there's a woman—single or not—who wouldn't mind landing a man like Gregory Caldwell. How someone hasn't locked him down already is beyond me. Still...

I want to ask more about Amelia and Silas. She's having none of that, as she launches into how Gregory pulled her over for speeding and somehow, they got to chatting and he asked her out. This seems typical of something that would happen to Amelia. Instead of a ticket, she got a date. It's also great to have another friend, one who isn't God knows where in the world.

Just as Amelia wraps up her gab session about her upcoming date, Chris, the bartender and owner, walks over to us.

"You ladies need anything?"

"Refills, please!" Amelia chirps. He nods and steps back to do just that. "Chris is a nice guy, too. I mean, if I get a little too carried away with my drinking and I'm alone, he'll fix me a cup of coffee and take me home. No funny business." A frown pinches her lips. "Can't decide if that's good or bad." She laughs, and then her eyes widen as if with an idea. "You should talk to him!"

I shake my head. "No, thanks. A break from men is what I need."

Amelia nods in understanding as Chris returns with fresh drinks. Guy chitchat over for the time being, we walk back to the table. We've been in our seats no more than two minutes before I hear my name. Instant recognition of who calls out for me causes my shoulders to sag.

Please go away.

They are the last people I want to talk to right now. It was only a matter of time before they all caught wind of what's happened and confronted me about it. Why did it have to happen here?

"Melanie, what is wrong with you?" It's Charlie, one of my older brothers.

"How could you leave Dad's when he's clearly upset

about what's going on?" Warren, my other brother and Charlie's paternal twin, adds.

"C'mon. We'll either drop you off at Dad's or you can come stay with one of us," Charlie informs me.

"I'm fine at home." Granted, I haven't been able to get much sleep unless Austin is there, but I'll never overcome my anxieties if I avoid my house altogether. Besides, I'd rather deal with my nerves than spend time with my family. I love them to death, but I'm so not in the mood.

"Someone vandalized and broke into your place," Warren unnecessarily points out.

"Yes, and? Someone replaced the door, painted it, and I now have a security system." I hate, hate, hate that this conversation is happening in front of other people, especially those I've only recently met. "Can we talk about this later? I'm fine. Honest."

Charlie gently grabs my arm. It's a complete contradiction to his words and tone. "Good Lord, Melanie. What do you know about replacing a door or security systems? Let's head over to your house so we can check what we need to fix." He tugs, but I swat at his hand. I've never been so embarrassed in my life.

"Why don't you leave her alone?" With a startled glance, I look over at Silas, who spoke up for me. "She said she didn't want to leave. You both need to back off. I think she's had enough assholes around lately without her own family bullyin' her."

The table falls silent at the fact that Silas stood up for me.

My brother's hand tightens and flexes on my arm. Charlie looks down at me with a glare. "What's he talkin' about? Has someone else been botherin' you? And where the fuck is Tyler in all this?"

Austin snorts at the mention of my ex. Unable to take this anymore, I nudge Charlie so I can stand and look back at Amelia. "I'm gonna head out with my brothers. Keep me posted on your date."

Between the little sleep I got last night, the long shift at work, and the clusterfuck of my brothers treating me like a child at the bar, I'm beat and over this day. They both pester me for answers as they follow me outside.

"Stop! Just fucking stop already!" I shout, whirling around to face them once we're close to my car. "Tyler and I broke up because he was hitting me, so please don't ask why he's not helping. I'm fine. I don't want to stay anywhere but at home, and that's what I'm going to do."

My brothers look devastated at my outburst.

Charlie steps forward to pull me into a hug. "We'll kick Tyler's ass." I sigh because I know they will, and that's the last thing I need. Not that they care what I truly need. "We're just worried. We don't want anything to happen to you. Dad said the vandalism happened while you were home, Melanie. You didn't even realize it."

"I know. I'm being more careful."

Warren steals me for his own hug. "Are you sure you don't want someone to stay with you? It'll make us feel better."

I shake my head. "I'll be fine." The idea of going home brings dread, but I'm hoping I'm too exhausted for my mind to keep me awake. I have to get over this at some point.

My brothers see me off thankfully, and I'm on my way, daydreaming of sweet dreams.

Hope is futile, though. Within minutes of lying down, it's as if a switch flips and I'm wide awake again. When will it get easier? Perhaps things will improve when I know I don't have to deal with whoever is angry with me.

Should I be upset that Austin didn't step in like Silas did? I don't think so. He said things between us wouldn't get complicated, and if he wants to keep Angela off my back, it is good he didn't defend me. I'm still shocked as shit that Silas did, though. I barely know him. Maybe he's that kind of guy.

My phone vibrates on my nightstand, and I reach over to grab it.

AUSTIN

Let me in. I know you're awake.

Feeling extreme relief that he's here and I won't have to sleep alone in this house should probably be a red flag, but I don't care. I rush downstairs, disarm the alarm, and open the door.

"Sorry it took me so long. I didn't want it to be obvious I was leavin' because of you." He locks the door behind him, waits for me to rearm the security system, and then takes my hand in his. "C'mon. You must be exhausted."

I am. I really am. This seems weird, though. For Austin to rush here because he knew I'd be too scared to sleep alone. He sheds his clothes and climbs in next to me as if we've done it a thousand times. Only tonight, he pulls me into his arms. His heart beats steadily beneath my ear, relaxing me.

"It won't always be like this. It'll get better," he whispers.

"Thanks, Austin. I'll bake you a cake on my next day off."

"You don't have to do that, but that's about all the argument you'll hear from me." I laugh at that. He squeezes my hip. "Get some rest, Mel."

Chapter Eight

Austin

I can't stay over tonight; Erin is here.
Amelia should be able to if you want to
call her.

MELANIE

About time I try it on my own, anyway. I
baked you a cake today. Is it okay if I walk
it over?

AUSTIN

Sure.

A few minutes later, there's a light rapping on the door. Erin glances at me in surprise. I walk over and open it. Melanie stands on the other side with the cake in her hands.

If it weren't for the fact that my daughter is in the room, I'd tell Mel I love her. This cake looks fucking delicious and smells it too. She hands it over, and I tilt my head for her to follow.

"Can't let you give me dessert without sharin' some

with you." To my daughter, I say, "Erin, you remember Melanie, right? She baked us a cake. Want a piece?"

She nods and follows me into the kitchen.

"I hope y'all like it. It's a new recipe I've been working on."

I cut each of us a slice, and then we sit at the table.

Erin hums in approval as she takes her first bite. "Can you teach me how to make this? I love to bake. Daddy and me bake something every time I come over."

"Sure, I'll give you the recipe."

I take a bite and moan, unable to help myself. This woman and her baking skills. I might need to seriously rethink my stance on relationships and this idea of being fuck buddies with Melanie. The cake tastes like a damn cinnamon roll.

My gaze locks on Melanie's. She's grinning from ear to ear, thrilled with our reactions. The woman needs to be a baker. Or maybe my personal baker? Either way works for me.

The cake is so delicious that the three of us finish it in silence.

Melanie sighs happily and then stands. "I should get going." Turning her gaze to Erin, she adds, "I'll make copies of my recipes and give them to your dad, okay?"

"Thanks!"

"I'll walk you out," I say as I stand. "Erin, why don't you go find a movie for us to watch?" She runs off to her room, where the movies are stashed. "Are you sure you'll be alright tonight?" I ask Melanie once Erin is out of earshot. Her being alone and unable to sleep has been on my mind entirely more than it should.

"Yeah. I hope so anyway. Enjoy the cake." She flashes a soft smile and then slips out of the front door.

It's tempting to sneak her in here if she has trouble, but I won't make that offer. That crosses whatever lines we've laid down since having sex. We need to keep things simple. Inviting her over here seems like the beginning of complicated.

Yet Melanie stays on my mind all night.

The next morning, I itch to message her to see how she slept, but I refrain. We've been friendly enough. Besides, today is full of activities, and Erin is all too eager to kick things off.

We are up early to meet Caleb at Go Ahead and Fry Me for breakfast. After talking to him at the diner the other day, it sounds like Angela is keeping Erin from him. I wasn't able to gain much from him before I realized Melanie had run off.

The plan is to spend most of the day with Caleb. If I can learn more about what's happening with him and Angela, even better. I absolutely refuse to put my daughter in the middle by questioning her. I need to know what's going on, though, especially since Angela isn't sharing.

After breakfast, we bring Erin to the park. Luckily, it's not too cold for her to play outside yet. One of her friends happens to be here as well, so Caleb and I take a seat on a nearby bench to watch her.

"I really appreciate this," he says. "Angela will be pissed when she finds out, though."

I shrug. "Erin calls you daddy too, and you're good to her. It's not right to kick you out of her life because of problems between you and Angela."

He thanks me again and then hesitates before he asks, "Has Erin said anything about what it's been like at Angela's lately?"

My shackles raise immediately. "She has asked why she

can't live with me and that she misses you. What's going on at home?"

Caleb sighs, his gaze on Erin. "Angela is dating someone, but I'm not sure who yet. I think he's been to the house, though, because I drove by the other day and a car was there. Other than the cheating, our problem has been that Angela drinks more than she should. One of the big reasons I didn't want to leave was because I didn't know how Erin'd fare alone with her."

Ice floods my veins. "You think she's not takin' care of her?"

"Not good enough at least. I can't prove it, though. Sorry. I've been trying to keep track of whatever I can that could help you gain full custody."

Erin runs over to ask Caleb to push her on the swings, so he gets up and follows her. Meanwhile, I'm frozen. If Caleb thinks I need custody, there's more going on than what he shared. Not once has he ever spoken a negative word about Angela and her parenting to me. I get it; she is his wife, soon-to-be ex-wife. But if my daughter had been suffering all this time, and he hadn't said...

Fuck. I need to ask Erin. How do I do that in such a way that she doesn't really know exactly what I'm asking? This stays on my mind all day. I wonder if I missed any signs from Erin that things are bad at home with Angela. I study her as if indications will turn up. As if I didn't already loathe the fact that I only see her every other weekend.

Caleb spends the whole day with us. We take Erin shopping as she apparently needs new cookie cutters, and she wants to bake some sugar cookies for Melanie in thanks for the cake. We take her to a museum and end our time together by spending a few hours at a local indoor pool. Erin loves to swim. She should've been a fish, really.

Later, after Erin changes into her pajamas, she finds me in the kitchen as I grab something to drink.

"Daddy?"

"Yeah, baby girl?"

She fidgets with the hem of her shirt. "Is Miss Melanie your girlfriend?"

I pause mid-pour. "Why do you ask?"

"Mom said she was."

At that, I clench my jaw and fight not to look pissed off. I put the pitcher back in the fridge.

"Well, is she? You like her a lot?"

"She is not my girlfriend. If I ever get one, I'll let you know, I promise. But Melanie is only our good neighbor." Another question filters out before I can stop it. "Do you like Melanie?" Why did I even ask?

Erin seems to contemplate my question seriously. "Yes," she replies decisively. "She's nice, and she's a good baker like me. Maybe the best baker ever."

"I agree, so let's keep being good neighbors to her, so she'll keep baking for us."

Erin smiles and nods. I set the glass down and take her hand to lead her to bed. Thank God that conversation is over.

Except...

"If you *do* get a girlfriend, would you forget about me?" There's an honest undercurrent of fear in her tone, which stops me in my tracks in the hallway outside of her room. "Mom said you might."

I will kill her! We need to have another talk, apparently.

With a deep breath, I crouch to be eye level with Erin.

Fuck, her eyes water, as if this has been something weighing on her lately.

"There is nothing, and no one, in this world that could

ever make me forget about you. You are my number one. Always. No matter what."

"Promise?"

"Promise."

Her shoulders sag in relief. She knows I keep my promises. She steps forward and throws her arms around my neck. "Love you, Daddy."

I hug her tight. "Love you too, baby girl. Now, let's get you to bed."

Erin is quick to fall asleep, and with the day calming, I can't help myself. This is becoming a sick obsession of sorts. I peer out one of my windows at Melanie's house. Fuck. All the lights are on. Movement catches my eye. Something stirs in my chest. Hope, perhaps? She's on her porch swing.

Without giving it a second thought, I snag my phone and slip out the front door, pulling up the app that shows the camera in Erin's room in case she wakes up.

Melanie startles as she hears my feet shuffling through the grass. She peers over her shoulder and relaxes as she sees me.

"Hey. How'd you fare?" I take a seat next to her.

She shrugs. "How was your day with Erin?"

I don't care for the non-answer and changing of subjects, but I let her have that for now. "It was good. Concerned about what it's like for her when she's with Angela, though." Melanie pins me with a questioning gaze, so I share what I found out from Caleb.

"Sorry, Austin. Silas is a cop, right? Maybe he can find dirt on her."

"That was a bust last time. She's careful." Unable to help myself any longer, I reach out and cup her jaw, lifting so I can better see her face. She looks exhausted. "You didn't sleep well," I state softly.

Her only response is a slight upturn of her lips. "I'm okay."

"Erin wants to make you sugar cookies in return for the cake, so I'll bring those over tomorrow after Angela picks her up. You may have incidentally started a bake war since you'll probably bake her something again as well."

Her smile lifts a little more. "She seems like a sweet kid. That's thanks to you, I'm sure."

I nod in agreement. "What brings you to the porch tonight?"

Melanie shrugs. "Just thinkin'."

When she doesn't elaborate, I decide not to push. Instead, I ask her about various things. We might as well be playing twenty questions as if we're on some sort of weird first date for how long we fire off questions at one another. At some point, Melanie rests her head on my shoulder.

Her talking has slowed a bit, stressing how tired she is, but I don't have the heart to stop her tale as she shares about her childhood.

"My parents divorced when I was five. At first, I didn't understand what was happening, but it was still okay. I got to see both my parents. But one day, my mom dropped me and my brothers off at my dad's, and I never saw her again. That's among the few memories I have of her.

"If my dad knows where she is, he's never said. She might as well be dead. I've never even thought of looking for her. My dad...he's a bulldog. He's pushy and overbearing and overprotective, but not once since she left has he ever made me feel as if I'm unloved or unwanted.

"He taught my brothers to be the same. To love fiercely and protectively. While they have tried their damnedest to take care of me, somewhere along the way, it was as if I was helpless without them. It screwed with me. Still does sometimes.

"I've always wanted to be a baker, but apparently, my mom was a great baker too. They seem horrified and terrified that I will become like her. Dad shut it down, and every time, he had something negative to say when I mentioned maybe opening a bakery in town. So I took his suggestion and chose a path that was more practical and helpful."

Melanie lifts her head and rubs her face. "Sorry. You only asked about my mom. I should lie down. I'm beat, and I have to be at work early." Before I can respond, Melanie stands and turns to look at me. She stares at me for what feels like forever. Maybe I'm crazy, but her eyes beg me to be a lifeline.

"What is it?"

She seems as if she wants to say one more thing. I'm oddly desperate to hear it.

"Nothing. Thanks for checking on me."

I stand and snag her hand before she can take a step. "Sweetheart. What is it?"

Melanie blinks slowly at me. It takes a second before I realize my mistake. Her name is Melanie or Mel. There should be no *sweetheart* bullshit. Melanie doesn't call me out on it. Instead, she asks a question of her own.

"Will you stop by tomorrow night?"

I squeeze her hand gently. "Sure." I don't know if she would like me to stay over so she can sleep better or if she wants to hook up. Surprisingly, I don't care which one it is.

Melanie lifts up and presses a kiss to the corner of my mouth. For some reason, it stuns me stupid. I stand there for another minute after she disappears inside before I finally head home. What in the world has this woman done to me?

"I've been thinking."

I keep the bitchy comments to myself. All I want Angela to do is get the fuck out, but Erin is in the kitchen putting the final touches on her cookie decorations, and Angela insisted on talking to me outside.

"We should get back together."

The moment her words register, I double over laughing, clutching my stomach. This is when I miss the look on Angela's face at my reaction.

I gather my wits and stop laughing. "You've got a better chance of being possessed by a demon than you do at us gettin' together."

"Austin—"

"Aren't you dating someone?"

Her lips press into a firm line. "No." I don't believe her, though. "Austin, listen to me. We were a good couple, and now that Caleb is out of the picture, we can put things back together between us. This would be great for Erin."

Fury surges through me. "Don't you dare bring her into this. Stop telling her I'm dating Melanie when I'm not. And speaking of Caleb, why are you keeping him from seeing her?"

Angela folds her arms across her chest. "Have you been talking to him?"

"Answer me."

"He's not her daddy." Angela takes a step closer to me, and she attempts to place her hand on my chest, but I step back before that can happen. "You are."

"You are the one who insisted she call him Daddy Caleb. He's been there her entire life. It's not right to keep her away from him because of whatever problems you two are havin'."

She ignores that completely. "Think about it, Austin. Caleb has stopped supporting us, and I'm stretched thin. Everything falls on me now. The mortgage, the bills, taking care of Erin. Two parents under one roof would give her stability."

This snake.

"This is about money then."

"It's about what's best for our family."

"We were never a family, Angela. You made sure of that when you fucked Caleb while I was deployed."

She rolls her eyes. "Let that go. I made a mistake, and I apologized for it."

"You never apologized. Not once. Us being together is good for no one. Nothing will change my mind on that."

"Just think about us, okay?"

The audacity of this woman. It's hard to fathom that I ever found her attractive, both personality-wise and physically.

"Never fucking happening."

"It is because of Melanie? Something is going on with you two."

"Maybe I'm not being clear enough. You could be the last woman on earth, and if it was between fuckin' you or sawin' my dick off with a dull knife, I'd happily take the knife and get to sawin'. It's. Never. Fucking. Happening."

The mask she wears, the one that hides the vileness living within her, slips. Rage, pure and ugly, twists her features. Just as quickly, she replaces it with a fake, sweet smile.

"You'll regret this, Austin. That girl next door is nothing but trouble, and you'll regret not choosing your family."

"Glad we're done here."

There's no point in acknowledging what is a veiled threat from Angela. I turn my back on her and step inside the house to officially end this ridiculous conversation. She's lost her marbles if she thinks I want to be with her again. The first time was bad enough. There won't ever be a second. I learned my lesson with crystal clarity.

Erin has finished her decorating, and Angela whisks her away. I set about cleaning up the mess she inevitably leaves behind. Like a pussy, my mind drifts to Melanie now that Erin is gone. I can't help but wonder how she's slept the past few days.

Once the house is all clean, I run out to grab us takeout, as she'll likely be hungry. I call in an order at Fry Me, which is ready by the time I arrive.

Mrs. Millie checks me out with an odd look on her face.

"What?" I finally ask.

"Are you seein' someone, sugar?"

I blink. "What?"

"This ain't your usual order when it's you and Erin, or you and Amelia. Just curious if you have some woman locked away that we don't know about."

I swallow hard and shake my head. It feels illegal to lie to the old lady, but I won't tell the truth either. Mrs. Millie continues to eye me as if she knows I'm lying through my teeth.

"You know who'd be a perfect match? That neighbor of yours. She's a sweet girl, isn't she? It's a downright shame all her baking talent is wasted. She does a nice thing, sure, but baking is her calling. You know, we've tried to convince her to bake our sweets, but she turns us down every time. Anyway, she'd be a good fit for you, don't you think?"

It's a relief that Mrs. Millie doesn't give me a chance to

answer. I'm barely keeping a straight face. Why does it feel as if I've been caught with my hand in the cookie jar?

"She needs a strong man to lift her up and support her independence." Her voice lowers. "That family of hers, God bless 'em, they love her, but they don't give her any breathing room." She tsks and then figuratively punches me in the gut as she gives me a once-over. "You know, maybe you aren't the right fit for her. I heard what Silas did for her at The Mad House." She nods to herself. "I'll put a little bug in his ear instead." Her gaze hits me. "Unless you think I shouldn't?"

"Got no problem with that, Mrs. Millie." Though, the idea of Silas and Melanie together makes me want to vomit.

She hums, making it more obvious she doesn't believe me. She hands over the bag of food. "Tell her I said hi, why don't you?"

I mutter a goodbye and haul ass out of there. Those old ladies are like a dog with a bone. If you're single and young, they seem to think they are matchmakers. They claim they know everyone well enough since practically all of Cardinal Point eats at their diner, anyway. They've been trying to set me up for years with no success.

Shaking off the encounter, I head home. By the time I make it back, Melanie's car is in the driveway. I walk over without delay.

I pause for a second when I see her front door isn't closed completely.

Pushing it open with my foot, I step inside and call out, "Mel?"

My heartbeat kicks up when there's no answer. It sounds like maybe her shower is running. I drop the food off in the kitchen and then jog upstairs to her room. The shower is definitely on.

"Melanie?" I shout from outside the bathroom door.

No response. My anxiety ratchets up.

"Melanie, I'm coming in."

I wait a beat to see if she will respond, but when she doesn't, I push the door open. Immediately, I rush over to her. She's sitting in her shower stall, leaning against one corner with her knees drawn up, her arms folded over the top, and her head resting on her arms.

"Melanie, sweetheart, are you okay?"

She lifts her blank gaze to me. I thought she was tired last night, but looking at her now in the harsh light of her bathroom, I realize I was wrong. The woman is absolutely exhausted.

"I just want to sleep," she mumbles.

"Christ, have you not slept at all?" I snatch a towel from the rack.

She shakes her head. "I wanted to shower first, but I'm so tired."

I bet she is. She hasn't slept since I was here on Thursday, and it's now Sunday night. I turn off the water, lean in to help her stand, wrap the towel around her, and then hold her hand as she steps out. She leans into me before we can take a step.

I hook my arm under her knees and pick her up. I barely make it five steps out of the bathroom before she stills and her breathing evens. She's not remotely dry. I lay her on the bed and pull the towel out from around her. My movements are automatic as I half-assedly pat her dry.

Her eyes pop open suddenly, and she sits up. "Austin?"

"Where are your pajamas?"

She falls back and rolls onto her side. "Who cares?"

Well, I most certainly do. There's no way I can lie next to her while she's naked and not lose a bit of my mind every single second of it. The idea of rummaging through her drawers makes me uneasy. Still, I walk over to her dresser, open the top drawer long enough to grab a pair of panties, and then shut it.

"Mel, help me quick, and then I promise you can sleep."

With a huff, she rolls onto her back. I've never dressed a grown woman before, and Melanie apparently doesn't care. For my sanity, she needs some clothes. I slip her underwear on and then yank my shirt off to pull it over her head. The moment I'm done, Melanie falls backward.

"You'll stay all night, right?" she asks with a yawn, her eyes never opening.

My chest warms at her question. "Yeah, sweetheart. Be right back."

After putting the food in the fridge, I return to her room, shed my pants and shoes, and climb in next to Melanie. She immediately wiggles over to press as tight against me as possible, snuggling into me.

"Thanks, Austin," she whispers.

I squeeze her hip. Within minutes, she settles and is asleep. I can't get over how heady of a fucking feeling it is to know that she feels so safe with me she's able to finally sleep after being unable to. It might be something I'm addicted to.

I'm in so much fucking trouble.

Chapter Nine

Melanie

M y alarm wakes me up, and I groan. I've not slept nearly long enough. Maybe after a week, I'll feel rested.

"Call in and take the day. I'll take off, too," Austin's gruff voice orders as I lean over to turn my alarm off.

If I were more awake, I'd probably argue. Instead, I shoot off a text to my boss and roll back over to snuggle against Austin. It takes less than a minute to fall asleep once more.

"If you don't stop."

My eyes flash open, and I calm my legs, which were rubbing together. My brain is still a bit foggy as I was having a fantastic sex dream.

"Awake now?" Austin asks, his voice rough with sleep.

"Yeah."

One second I'm lying on my side beside him, and the

next, he has me on my back, my shirt is over my head, and he slips my panties off. He runs his hands over my legs and then parts them. My breath catches as he lowers his mouth.

I'm not sure what happened for Austin to grace me with his tongue between my thighs, but I won't complain. Nor do I when after I orgasm, he climbs up my body and thrusts into me. Every morning should start with multiple orgasms. I'd be so much more motivated to tackle the day.

Austin is a fantastic partner in bed, too. He talks dirty to me, which I like more than I thought I would. And his hands. Good lord. He is constantly moving. Running over my skin, playing with my breasts, diving into my hair. I'm here for it.

Taking him up on this friends with benefits offer might be the best thing to happen all year.

After he gives me two more orgasms, I'm so spent, I fall back to sleep.

Sometime later, I wake up to the smell of coffee. Austin is no longer in bed, so I reluctantly get up, make a stop by the bathroom, and then mosey on downstairs after wrapping a robe around me.

Austin is pouring himself a cup when I walk into the kitchen. He throws me a smile over his shoulder.

"Sleep well?"

I nod. My stomach clenches at the reminder that I wasn't able to get any shuteye while home alone. How much longer must this terrorize me?

"Hey, what's wrong?" Austin sets a mug in front of me and then sits next to me.

"I think I'm gonna have to move somewhere else," I quietly admit with my eyes cast on my coffee. "I don't feel safe here anymore. During the day, it's easier to ignore because I can keep myself busy, but at night?" I shake my head as shame and embarrassment fill me. "The only way I'm sleeping is if you're here. I can't keep asking you to come over, and you can't always be here. I think I need to sell it and stay with my dad or one of my brothers in the meantime."

When Austin says nothing, I lift my gaze. He doesn't look thrilled, but then again, his face is pretty blank.

"Whatever you think is best," he finally replies.

Well, I certainly can't endure another weekend without sleep while having to work. My gaze wanders over to the clock on the stove, and I see it's well into the afternoon. An entire day wasted on catching up on rest.

"Thanks for taking the time off with me," I say, focusing back on Austin. "I'm good if you have other things to do."

Things are a bit weird between Austin and me; I'm not too sure what to do about it or if I even have the capacity. This strictly friends with benefits thing may not be working out. I'm relying on him entirely too much, and he's calling me sweetheart.

Before he can respond, my phone rings with a call from my father. I excuse myself and step into the living room.

"Daddy—"

He immediately cuts me off. "What's wrong? Why aren't you at work?"

I roll my eyes so hard I'm surprised they don't pop out. *Of course,* he somehow found out I wasn't working today.

"I just needed a day. I'm glad you called, though."

"What do you need? Do you want to come stay here? Or I can send Warren and Charlie over. Has something else happened? Melanie, dear, you should really let one of us look after you."

"Daddy," I say when he takes a breath, but it's no use.

"We're rightly worried, you know. You shouldn't be in

that house all alone. I understand you're protected as well as you can be, but it'll be better if you had someone there to look after you."

I tune out as my shoulders sag. My family loves me more than anything—I know this—but they smother me. If I stay with my dad, it won't be long until he inadvertently starts making me feel incompetent. It's like he harbors guilt that he didn't do enough for Mom, and that's why she left. Somehow, he feels as if he has to be so helpful to the point he ends up causing me to feel like I'm incapable of doing it on my own. He means well, I honestly believe he does, but if it's between living here and not sleeping or staying with my dad, it's unfortunately an easy decision.

Just as I'm about to interrupt my dad to assure him that I'll stay at his house, fingers wrap around my wrist, causing my eyes to open.

"Stay," Austin whispers. "We'll work something out."

Something in his gaze makes my belly do a flip. Like he knows it'll be as stressful—just in a different way—for me to stay with my father. Like he can't bear the thought of not being the one to help me. It's the look—which sends a shiver through me—that causes me to interrupt Dad.

"That's why I was calling, Daddy. I wanted to ease your worries. A friend is staying with me, or I'll be staying with her. I'm okay."

Austin graces me with a soft smile and then kisses my temple before leaving me to have some privacy once again. I let my dad rattle on for a few minutes longer before stating I needed to go.

When I return to the kitchen, Austin is placing two takeout containers on the table.

"Heated up the supper I bought last night," he explains before continuing on. "I was thinking. I don't mind stayin' here or you stayin' at my house. When Erin is over, Amelia can come instead, or vice versa. If we absolutely had to, I could sneak you in once she's asleep."

Part of me wants to protest bringing Amelia into this. I can't do that, though, without sharing why I would rather not bother Amelia. She has a life. She goes on her date with Gregory soon, and if that doesn't work out, then there's Silas.

My phone vibrates, and I check my messages.

IZZY

My best friend alarm has been going off.
I'm coming home to stay with you. Be there
tomorrow. No objections, because I'm
already on my way.

And now I want to cry. Izzy and I connected a long time ago in high school at our book club. She left within weeks of graduation to work for a cruise line. Earlier this year, she quit that job and has been traveling across the continental US while continuing a business she started while she was still working on the cruise ship. We've met up a few times over the years. I always go to her because Izzy avoids Cardinal Point.

The friendship we had in high school was ironclad. Even though we might not talk as much as before with all the things happening in our lives, we pick up where we left off when we reconnect. We are pillars of strength for one another. She for me because she was always there when things got to be too much with my family. Me for her as her life fell apart in high school and then she struggled with both a long-distance sort of relationship and her new family dynamics.

She'd stayed gone all this time because she is terrified to face what may wait for her here. Or what isn't.

The fact that she is returning to Cardinal Point for me?

"Hey, what's the matter?" Austin asks softly as he reaches out to wipe a fallen tear.

"My best friend is coming home to stay with me. I didn't realize how much I missed her and needed her until just now."

Austin lifts one corner of his mouth. "See? It'll all work out."

I shoot a quick text back to her that I can't wait and then dive into the food Austin brought.

"Thank you," I tell him.

"If you really want to thank me, you can bake somethin' for me."

At that, I laugh. "Any requests?"

He shakes his head. "Surprise me, sweetheart. Everything you've made so far has taken me to my knees, ready to propose. I still need to buy a ring and convince you to agree."

A stream of giggles leaves me at that. And they say women are dramatic. The way he goes on about my baking is silly, but I love it so much. I regularly bake for others I meet and know around town, but no one showers me with praise quite like Austin. Plus, since it unnecessarily freaks my father out, I can't share it with them unless it's a baking-appropriate time like the holidays.

"Do you enjoy being a paramedic? Like, are you happy you do that instead of baking full-time?"

I contemplate his question as I poke at my food, not entirely hungry anymore. "I love helping people, yes," I finally answer, avoiding his gaze.

Austin only hums in response.

We spend the rest of the afternoon together. Austin ventures out to grab some ingredients so I can bake him something as promised. It's odd how easy things are between us. Perhaps it's because we're not in a relationship, so there's no pressure. We're friends. Just neighbors. It's not complicated.

Having him in my kitchen, *helping* me bake, though? I swear, I have a mini-orgasm. He has never been more attractive to me than rolling out dough, flour dusting his hands, and cracking a total dad joke that apparently got Erin in a fit of giggles last he saw her.

The moment the dessert is in the oven, I grab his hand. I'm a bit ashamed to say we didn't even make it out of the kitchen fully before I attacked and we had some of the hottest sex yet.

All because he baked with me.

The sound of a phone ringing rouses me awake.

"Baby girl, what's wrong?"

I sit up, immediately alert, and listen to Erin reply in a shaky tone, "I had a nightmare and Mom's not here. I know I'm not supposed to call you when she leaves, but I'm scared to go back to sleep. Can you come get me?"

Austin sits with his legs already over the edge of the bed, and since his phone isn't to his ear, I'm guessing she did a video call. His body locks up at what Erin says.

"Your mom's not there?" She must shake her head because he follows up with, "She's left you alone before?" And then, "You checked everywhere?"

"And I tried to call her, but she didn't answer."

"Okay. Hang tight. I'm going to put the phone down and turn the video off for just a second, so I can change my clothes, but I won't hang up until I'm there, okay?"

"Okay," she whispers.

Austin places his cell on the bed and stands, letting out a string of curses as he dresses. He looks over his shoulder at me.

"I've gotta go. You gonna be alright? I'll let you know when I'm back in case you want to come over."

I shake my head, realizing he must've also muted the call. "No, I'll be okay. Don't worry about me. Let me know if you need anything, though."

"I need to travel back in time and never go on that damn date with Angela. She's going to lead me to an early death."

"Daddy?"

At Erin's voice, he grabs his phone and unmutes it. "Still here. I'm on my way out the door as soon as I put on my shoes. Give me one more minute." He's already rounding the bed. He stops, leans over, and places a soft kiss on my mouth. "I'll check on you tomorrow, sweetheart."

Once I nod, he's gone.

Chapter Ten

Austin

The moment I'm in front of Angela's door, Erin unlocks it from her side, opens it, and we disconnect the call. I give her a long hug. Even though I know she's not hurt, I can't help but look her over anyway.

"Got your bag for school ready?"

She nods and runs to grab it from next to the couch. I step inside, take it from her, and with my phone recording, walk through Angela's house to confirm she's not here. Her car isn't here, and Erin said she looked, so I'm not surprised.

As I was walking out of Melanie's house, I turned screen capture on my phone so it would record my conversation with Erin. Angela's fucked up, and I'm sure as hell taking advantage of it. I probed her again to have her repeat the fact that she was home alone, and this wasn't the first time.

Apparently, since Caleb left, this has been happening. Sometimes on the weekends, mostly at night.

"Am I going to get in trouble, Daddy?" she asks, the tremble clear in her tone.

As gently as possible, I talk to my daughter. "No, baby

girl, you're not gonna be in trouble. I know Mom asked you not to call me and you did what she said, but movin' forward, if *anyone* asks you to do *anything* that makes you feel bad or you don't like, you tell me, or your teacher, or your nana, or Daddy Caleb, anyone you feel safe with. Okay?"

"Okay, Daddy," she whispers.

We're quiet until I pull into my driveway and Erin quietly asks, "Do I have to go back to Mom's?"

"Do you want to?" Not that I'm allowing it, but I would like to know her response.

"No, I wanna live with you."

"Daddy's going to make that happen." It's another promise I'll keep.

Even from the front seat, her exhale of relief is audible. Yeah, Angela and I are gonna have a long fucking talk. My lawyer is getting an email before I fall asleep too and then a call first thing in the morning.

As we step out of the truck, I can't help but glance at Melanie's place. My gut twists at seeing her bedroom light on. Nothing I can do about that right now. I get Erin inside and settled, though I have to lie with her until she dozes off, before I head to my room.

After I email my lawyer, my phone pings with a text.

MELANIE

I couldn't sleep after you left, worrying about Erin. She sounded pretty scared. Is she okay?

Hopefully, you're not already asleep, and my message wakes you up. Just wanted to ask since I saw you were home.

AUSTIN

She's okay. Expect Angela will be here first thing.

Do you think you'll be able to go back to sleep? You can come over.

I fucking love that she's worried about my little girl, though I'm sure that's not the only reason she could not fall back to sleep. It takes about ten minutes before Melanie texts me again.

MELANIE

Are you sure?

AUSTIN

Wouldn't have mentioned it if I wasn't.

MELANIE

On my way over.

I leave my bedroom and open the front door just as Melanie steps onto my porch. After snagging her hand, we walk to my room. I'm not too worried about the morning; she leaves for work early.

"Thank you, Austin." The sincerity in her voice overwhelms me.

I don't respond. I pull her onto the bed with me and into my arms. She's hooked her claws into me; there's no denying it at this point. The surprising part is I've continued to allow it. That is something to think about another day.

"Get some rest," I murmur as I press a kiss to the top of her head.

106

In the morning, Angela has the misfortune of arriving at my house after Erin and I have already left. She simply sends a text to confirm Erin is with me and then says she'd come over after work to explain and pick Erin up.

The one thing she *will not do* is pick Erin up. I told my daughter she isn't going back to her mother's, and I meant it. Therefore, Amelia will pick Erin up from school, and she'll hang with her until I get Angela sorted.

Work is a bit of a pain. My front desk clerk, Stacey, is in a perky mood. She pops into my office seconds behind me, and hands over a coffee.

"You really don't have to make me coffee." I'd rather she didn't, honestly.

"It's no big deal. I brought some goodies in today. Apple pie, chocolate chip cookies, and brownies. All from Bake My Day, so you know it'll be delicious."

I've had apple pie from Bake My Day. It's good, but Melanie's? Better. "Thanks. I'm sure the guys will appreciate the sugar boost." This doesn't make me nearly as uncomfortable, if only because she includes everyone.

"If you'll let me know when you're ready for a slice of the pie, I'll bring it to you."

"Ah, thanks, but I'm good. I've had a lot of sweets lately, so I should probably skip this round."

Her face falls for a second before the disappointment disappears. "Oh. Okay. Maybe next time. I'll let you get to work then."

She ducks out, and I focus on all I need to accomplish today. Mostly consultations. The day is slow until one of our machines throws a fit and seems to breathe its last breath. It's just the kind of day where everything annoys me and nothing seems to run smoothly.

To be fair, I've been in a bad mood since Angela texted this morning. Knowing I'll have to deal with her later gives me both pleasure and dread. She never makes anything easy. I doubt today will be the day she changes her tune.

Ultimately, I'm home from work for half an hour when Angela knocks on my door. I step out onto the porch to keep her out of my house. Angela immediately narrows her eyes at me.

"Well?" I ask when she doesn't readily provide an explanation. "What godforsaken reason do you have for abandoning our child at home alone at night? Let's hear it."

"She was fine, Austin. She's old enough to—"

"Just stop. If all you're going to do is spout bullshit, then go home. Erin is stayin' here until we get new custody papers drawn. You told our seven-year-old not to tell anyone she was by herself. You knew it was wrong! What the fuck is the matter with you?"

A car pulls into Melanie's and distracts me for a moment, especially when I see it's not her friend who is returning to town. It's Tyler. As Angela launches into her spiel about why her actions were perfectly reasonable, I try my best to turn nonchalantly, leaning my back against the edge of the doorframe, and keep my gaze in Melanie's general direction.

My body tenses as he gets out of his car, slams his door shut, and barrels with fury in his entire being toward her front porch. Angela is so interested in telling her story, she doesn't even pause as Tyler bangs on Melanie's door.

Don't answer, Melanie. Don't fucking answer.

But this is the woman who loves to stress the shit out of

me because she teeters on the line between safety and stupidity.

Of course, she opens the door. I think it's her goal to be the one who gives me gray hairs instead of Erin.

It takes Tyler all of a breath to grab her by the throat and slam her against the wall of her house. The ability to stay out of it snaps so quickly and loudly, I'm surprised the entire world doesn't hear it. My body moves before I fully realize it.

"Austin! Where are you going?" I vaguely perceive Angela shouting at me.

There's a roar in my ears as Tyler yells in her face, "Did you seriously have those fucking goons you call brothers come after me?"

As I step onto Melanie's porch, my vision turns red. Not only does he have her pinned as her hands scratch at his arm, but he has her lifted just enough that her toes barely touch the floor. I know this because her terrified eyes meet mine over his head.

Without thinking, I yank him away by the shoulder and throw a punch. He goes down and I follow, straddling him as I land three more punches. What kind of fucking man lays his hand on a woman?

It's not until there's a hard pull on my shirt, unbalancing me, that I snap out of it. The red disappears, and the roar ceases as I hear, "Austin! Stop!"

I release the pathetic excuse of a human being, get to my feet, and turn to find a still terrified Melanie.

"You okay?"

There's blood on her lip! I nearly lose my shit again. When the fuck was he able to hit her?

Before Melanie can answer, Tyler groans and pulls himself to his feet.

"She sent her brothers after me!" As if that's an acceptable reason to attack her.

I grab him by the throat and pin him like he did her. "Listen to me carefully. You come here again, you get within five feet of her, you do *anything* she doesn't like, and," I lean in until my eyes are all he can see, "I will *ruin* you. You won't be able to work, shop, or show your stupid fucking face in this town without feeling my wrath."

I expect him to spout off at me, but he must see something in my eyes because he remains silent.

"You understand?"

He nods.

I release him, and he scurries off Melanie's porch, muttering under his breath. I turn to her again, my hands cupping her face.

"You okay?" I ask gently once more.

She whispers, "I told them not to do it. I hoped they wouldn't."

I don't give a shit about her brothers or what they did to Tyler. "Are. You. Okay?"

She nods. I finally breathe a sigh of relief. My eyes close, and I rest my forehead against hers.

"No more opening the door without checking who it is first."

Melanie nods again.

"Are you two done now?"

Both of us turn to stone. Fucking Angela. Melanie takes a step away from me, and my hands fall. The fucked-up part is Melanie looks apologetic.

"I'll check in on you later," I tell her softly before I hurry down the steps and walk past Angela back to my porch.

Angela follows after me, right on my heels. "So you *are*

fucking the neighbor. Have you lost your mind, Austin? That woman does nothing but attract drama and trouble. Our daughter doesn't need to be exposed to whatever she has going on."

"Our daughter?" I laugh humorlessly. "You've made it clear you don't have Erin's best interests in mind."

"What are you talking about? I always have her best interests at heart!" If I didn't know her better, didn't know how good of an actress she could be, I'd think there was genuine belief and distress in her tone. "I've made mistakes," she admits. "But we can be a family again, Austin."

"Not on your life," I retort as I almost reach my porch steps.

Her tone turns nasty. "If you think my daughter—"

I whirl on her and get in her face without touching her. Absolute venom dominates my tone. "If you think *my* daughter is going to be left alone in *your* care again, you've lost *your* fucking mind, Angela. Erin's staying. You're leaving Melanie out of it. End of."

Before she can respond, I storm into my house, slamming the door and locking it to ensure she doesn't follow.

"This isn't over, Austin!" she shouts from the other side.

Once I hear her car door closing, I release a loud and long, "Fuuuuccccckkk!"

The absolute last thing we needed was for Angela to find out. Melanie thought her life sucked before today? Angela is sure to make it even worse.

It's not until later that two terrifying thoughts hit me: What if Melanie wants to cut ties to avoid Angela's bullshit? What if I don't want her to?

Chapter Eleven

Melanie

It's been an hour since the drama outside my house. Izzy only got here fifteen minutes ago and settles in while I arrange our takeout on the coffee table.

A knock raps against the front door, startling me for a moment. I walk over and use my peephole. The tension leaves my body as I see Austin.

I pull the door open. With one hand in his pocket, the other extends toward me.

"Know you got company, sweetheart. You got a minute to spare for me?"

"Be right back, Izzy," I call without looking and take his hand.

Austin leads me over to the swing, sits, braces his legs, and pulls me until I straddle his lap. For a moment, he says nothing. He simply runs his palms from my shoulders, down my arms, down my thighs, and then back up again until his hands settle on my hips.

"You still okay?" At my nod, he continues. "You don't have to say anything. You have company, and I need to pick

Erin up, but I need to get this out and for you to listen and mull it over."

I give him another nod. My stomach knots itself over and over, wondering what bad news he's about to lay on me.

"You've got a lot on your plate right now. This thing between you and me shouldn't have added to that. It was supposed to be the opposite. With Angela seein' me over here today, it's not good. I think with her fuck-up, she won't threaten me with Erin for the time being, so the bigger issue is how she's goin' to be toward you.

"Last woman I truly liked even a little, thinkin' she may be worth dealin' with Angela's bullshit, Angela knew it. She came at me, but she also went after her. By that, I mean she harassed her online. Told her lies. Showed up and made a scene in public, including at the woman's job. Though I couldn't prove it, I think she keyed her car, too."

My eyes widen at that, and Austin squeezes my hips once.

"I'm sayin' all of this because something's going on with Angela and more than usual; I don't know where her mind is. There's no telling how she's gonna react or what she's going to do, especially since she's made it known to me she wants me back. She's gonna think you are the reason I said no."

His fingertips dig into my skin. "Think on that. See if you want to add this to your plate until I can figure out how to get free of her enough to breathe easy for the first time in years."

His grip loosens as his hands lightly glide upward until he's cupping my face. His voice lowers, and his gaze pierces mine. "For what it's worth, hope you'll be willing to hold that extra weight for a bit. Not sure when exactly it happened or how, but startin' to think I was good with just fuckin' women in quiet because I've been waitin' for someone who's worth the fall."

Austin lets that hang in the air, his eyes telling me he thinks I'm worth taking the risk on. Pleading for me to fall too. That's all crazy talk. He must mean something else. We're only friends.

"Think it was your bakin'."

At that, I laugh, and he gives me a small grin.

"That's all, sweetheart. I know you've got your girlfriend in there and will be good, but I'm still next door, no matter what."

"Can I get a kiss before you go?"

His small grin turns into a big one. He answers by giving me my kiss. A hot, wet, long kiss that leaves me breathless when he pulls away and pats my thigh.

"I'm gonna get Erin. Text me later after you've caught up with Izzy."

I stand and nod. "We'll gossip about you," I warn, making him laugh.

"Have fun then." He gives my hand one more squeeze, nods toward my door, and waits until I've stepped inside to leave.

"You haven't mentioned a new man. How dare you?" Izzy teases as I shut the door behind me. "What happened to Tyler?" She takes a seat on the couch, and I follow suit.

I launch into all the gritty details I didn't share the last few times we've communicated. By the time I'm finished, Izzy pulls me into a hug.

"I'm glad I came, and I'm even more glad you are free of Tyler. I never met him, but I had a bad feeling about him."

All talked out about my life, I move us along. "How are *you*? How is it being back in Cardinal Point when you're trying to avoid the love of your life?"

Izzy rolls her eyes, but her shoulders slump. "We go through these spells where we don't talk much. In one now because he's seeing someone. Sometimes, I wonder if it's because we're both trying to move on and it doesn't feel right to talk to one another, which just makes it harder to move on. For me at least, because I know if it doesn't work out, he'll be there. Unless he ends up getting married or something," she finishes quietly.

"Why don't you let him know you're in town and meet up?" I ask, though I am aware of the reason. They were supposed to meet once, but Eric bailed on her. Ever since, neither has mentioned it.

Izzy is quiet for a moment before she sighs. "He's seeing someone," she reminds me. "And it's been years, Melanie. He's always been the one to take that first step, and he hasn't. What does that tell you?"

"Maybe he's waiting for you to take the step since he messed up last time when he offered to meet," I gently suggest.

"Can't do anything about it now."

That's true. If he's seeing someone, it's best Izzy leaves him alone.

"Do you think you'll ever move back? Or do you want to be a nomad all your life? Are you going to see your family while you're here?"

"God, no," she answers my last question first. "I don't plan to leave your house unless I absolutely need to. I'm here for *you*. As far as moving back, I don't know." Izzy sighs. "I kind of want to," she admits quietly. "Seeing the States is nice and I've enjoyed it, but that feeling I got when I saw the town limits?" She shakes her head. "I ached to move back."

I wish she would. It needs to be on her own time, though. Just then, my phone vibrates with a text.

> **AMELIA**
>
> Austin said your long-lost bestie is back in town. Sounds like we need to have an alcohol-filled slumber party Friday. I'm crashing your bonding time regardless, so let me know if I should pack a bag too.

"That your new man?" Izzy asks, probably noting my smile.

"No, his sister. Amelia. She wants to come over and meet you on Friday. Are you okay with that? She's good people."

"Yeah, sure. It sounds fun."

Let's just hope the time between now and then gives no more surprises.

Austin wasn't lying when he said Angela would be a problem. She has entirely too much time on her hands. Somehow, she got ahold of my number and started blowing up my phone with crazy texts.

> **ANGELA**
>
> Hey, it's Angela. I just wanted to reach out and let you know that while you and Austin have this little thing going on, we're actually discussing getting back together. Seems inappropriate for you to continue on with him when we're trying to put his family back together.
>
> So, are you going to take a step back?

Really? No response? I'm just trying to help you out. If people find out you're messing around with him like this, that's going to bite you in the ass. No one likes a home wrecker keeping a family separated.

You know, you're a stupid bitch if you think Austin sees a future with you. OR if you think I'd allow some skank around my daughter. If you need dick that bad and like sloppy seconds, I can send my soon-to-be ex-husband your way.

On and on it went until I finally blocked her without ever responding.

Then, the crazy woman started *emailing* me. How she got my email, I don't know.

These remained unacknowledged as well.

As if that wasn't enough, when I finish my shift a few days later, I find her in the parking lot of the hospital I work out of, leaning against my car with her arms folded.

It's a miracle I'm able to withhold my sigh.

"Since you're intent on ignoring me, I thought I'd show up so we can have a little chat," she says once I'm close enough.

"I'm ignoring you because you're out of line and harassing me. We have nothing to discuss."

"You're seeing Austin." There's disgust in her tone, and her face scrunches up to match. "You're in the way of putting my family back together."

I laugh. "You're delusional. Your family is broken because of *you*, not me. If Austin doesn't want to start something back up with you, that's not on me."

"He doesn't want to be with me because he's with you!" She throws her arms up in exasperation.

I shake my head. "Austin had no intention of getting

back together with you before he was with me. And Austin and I aren't even together. He's just my neighbor."

At this, she raises an eyebrow at me. It's not my fault she doesn't believe me. As far as I know, we *aren't* together. We're still friends with benefits. He has only asked that I don't jump our friends-with-benefits ship with the crazy in Angela coming out to play.

When he talked to me earlier this week on my front porch, none of that translated into us dating.

Right?

Did I miss something?

I mean, he mentioned something about me being worth dealing with her, but that doesn't mean things changed.

Does it?

No, no, definitely not. Austin was so genuinely honest when he said he wanted to keep things simple and easy. Nothing has happened for him to change his mind.

"For what it's worth, hope you'll want to hold that extra weight for a bit. Not sure when exactly it happened or how, but startin' to think I was good with just fuckin' women in quiet because I've been waitin' for someone who's worth the fall."

That's the part that gives me pause, but not enough to abandon the friends with benefits relationship and start thinking about an actual romantic one. It was a stressful day. He was delirious or something.

Angela doesn't believe me either, apparently. "He ran over, hit and threatened Tyler, and then—"

"He was concerned, as anyone would be," I interrupt. "Look, if you want to be upset that Austin is unavailable to you, then go ahead. I understand. I haven't known him all that long, but I can see he's a good man. A good man *you* fucked over and lost. Comin' after me is just gonna piss him off and make that canyon between you even bigger. You have a daughter—"

The slap comes fast and *hard*, causing me to lose my footing a bit and take a step back. My cheek stings and burns.

"Don't you dare bring my daughter into this."

I'm officially done. "Don't bring *me* into this. You have something to say about me being in Austin's life, take it up with him." I walk around her and get in my car. It takes more restraint than I thought it would not to run her over in the process.

No wonder Austin doesn't want to date. She's a piece of work. Today wasn't half bad considering the messages she sent. Something tells me she's just getting started, though.

The rest of the week goes smoothly enough, I guess. Since Izzy doesn't want to spend time in public, we've crashed at my place. I've actually been able to relax a little more with her here. Austin texts me fairly often. Izzy and I even had dinner with him and Erin once.

Tonight, Amelia is coming over, and I'm really excited about it. It's also Halloween, and instead of candy, I've spent all day baking cookies to give out. Unfortunately, no one has stopped by, and I'm a little depressed by it.

There's a knock on the door, and I answer, expecting Amelia.

I'm absolutely delighted to find Erin dressed as a baker with Austin a few steps behind her, leaning against my porch railing.

"Trick or treat!" Erin greets.

"Well, look at you! Love the costume, Erin."

"Thank you," she chirps.

I grab the platter of sweets and hold it out to her. Her eyes widen.

"Cookies!" she squeals. "Thank you!" She grabs one and then adds, "Can my daddy have one?"

"Absolutely. In fact, you can have all of them."

Erin gasps and whirls around to face Austin.

"Melanie, we don't need all the cookies," he tells me.

"Well, since no other kids showed up and Erin did; you're getting them."

Erin begs her dad, but his eyes remain glued to mine for what feels like an eternity until they drop to his daughter.

"Half of them," he barters. "Aunt Amelia is coming over to Melanie's tonight, and she'll be sad if there are none left for her."

Taking that for the victory it is, I advise I'll be back. After packing up half the cookies and a little surprise, I return and drop it in her plastic pumpkin.

"Thanks, Miss Melanie!"

"Any time. I tossed in my recipe for pumpkin pie too."

Erin squeals in excitement and Austin cuts in.

"Alright, baby girl. Let's head home."

I wave as they walk next door.

Within the hour, Amelia arrives and we're chowing down on pizza. Amelia and Izzy have been gabbing a bit, learning about one another, with me chiming in here and there.

Until Amelia turns her attention to me.

"Are you seein' my brother?"

I nearly choke on my beer at her blunt question.

"Ah, how did the date with Gregory go?" I ask instead.

"Ah, ah, ah. My question first, though I can guess by

your non-response that you are." She doesn't seem upset, which is good.

I hesitate for a moment before admitting the truth. "We're like you and Silas."

"Who's Silas?" Izzy asks.

"One of Austin's friends and Amelia's fuck buddy," I reply. "That is, if things didn't go well with Gregory Caldwell."

Izzy hums. "A date with the town's most wanted bachelor. Lucky you."

Amelia sighs. "Yeah, well, apparently he isn't it for me. How a man that fine can kiss so damn good and there still not be a spark, I don't know. Silas is stuck with me a bit longer. But," she shifts her gaze to me, "you need to stop changin' the subject. What's going on with you and Austin?"

"The same as you and Silas," I repeat. "We're friends who occasionally fuck." At that, Amelia frowns in disgust. "I've had some trouble sleeping alone since someone broke into my house, and he stayed over to help me sleep. It's nothing serious."

The disgust leaves, but the frown remains. "I wish I didn't know this, but Silas thinks it's more than that because my brother hasn't fucked the same woman twice since Angela."

That I didn't know. Do I want to dwell on that? I don't think so. "Well, I'm not sure what to tell you. We're just friends."

"Are you happy with that?"

The question comes from Izzy, which surprises me.

"Why don't you tell her about *your* man?" I ask.

"What if he wants more?" Amelia says, her tone suddenly serious. When I simply stare at her in surprise, she

121

continues, "It's been a long time since my brother wanted more from a woman and if he *does* want more with you, but you *don't*, then I think you need to end it now before he gets hurt. So, are you interested in more?"

My mouth opens and closes a few times before I'm able to settle on my answer. "Austin has been a really good friend to me, but like with Silas, he expressed what he wanted from this. I don't want to think of anything else when I don't know with one hundred percent certainty what he wants."

She nods in understanding. We spiral from there, talking about current love interests and old ones as we eat and drink. At some point, we play a card game, spilling our secrets, while demolishing the extra goodies I baked for us.

"What's something no one else knows about you? Like no one close to you?" Amelia asks. Each of us has been posing a question that all three of us have to answer.

"Well, that's easy," Izzy says. "Only Mel knows about Eric."

Amelia waves her off as she throws down her card. "Doesn't count. Has to be no one."

Izzy falls silent, her gaze moving between us, before she whispers, "Someone proposed to me once."

"*What?*" I screech. "When? Who? Oh, my God. Are you actually married?"

She shakes her head quickly. "That long-time boyfriend I had?" I nod. "He did."

"You turned him down because of Eric?" Amelia guesses.

Izzy nods with a bit of shame. "He was all I could think about. I felt horrible. Marshall was a great guy, and I fucked him over. I haven't dated since."

Amelia's eyes widen. "But you're hooking up, right?"

"Not even that."

Amelia whistles in disbelief. I reach over to rest my hand on Izzy's. "You could've told me," I tell her. "If only to lean on me."

She shrugs and moves us along by asking what mine is. I don't have many secrets that at least one person doesn't know. Austin knows I used to dream of being a baker, and so does Izzy. My brothers are aware that I have long since abandoned the idea of wanting to find out more about my mother. Except...

"Once after I turned eighteen, I met with a private investigator. There was a time, like a month after I graduated, when I couldn't stop thinking about my mom, and I was going to ask him to find her. I chickened out, though. I felt so guilty after all my brothers and dad have done for me. It didn't feel right. I don't regret it."

Izzy gives me an understanding look and also mentions how I could've told her about that. After a minute, we both turn to Amelia, who has gotten surprisingly quiet. She looks between the two of us and then whispers her confession.

"I was sort of assaulted in college by a professor."

"Sort of?" Izzy questions, outrage already in her tone.

Amelia swallows hard, avoiding our gaze. "There was some unwanted kissing and minor touching."

"Minor?" Izzy exclaims. "What the fuck? Amelia, you don't have to downplay that. I'm sorry it happened to you."

Amelia shrugs.

"How come your family doesn't know this?"

At this, her gaze lifts to mine. "No one believed me when I reported it at school. They removed me from his class, and that was that. I never brought it up again."

Both of us stare in stunned silence at her.

"We clearly need more liquor. I'm going to bother your

brother and see what he has." Izzy stands and walks out of the house.

"Amelia," I start, unsure what even to say.

"It's fine. I'm good." She plasters the fakest smile I've ever seen on her face. "Just gets to me sometimes that they took his side."

"There is no side, Amelia. Yours is the truth, and that's the only side. They were assholes, and hopefully, they'll burn in hell for how they treated you."

"We can hope."

After that, our twenty questions confessional session is over as soon as Izzy returns with a bottle of wine that Austin keeps stashed for Amelia at his place. Before long, we're all laughing and stumbling around.

It's been ages since I've had good girl time. Already, I hate that Izzy will leave soon. While she misses being home, she's been antsy to jump ship ever since she heard from Eric, who got into a fight with his latest girlfriend. She'll be gone shortly, which is fine. She has to live her life. I just wish she were ready to move home.

For now, we're going to drink, eat, and gossip our hearts out.

Chapter Twelve

Austin

Erin is with Caleb and his parents this weekend. My lawyer was able to get me temporary full custody because of statements from Erin while we wait for a permanent change. It's been over a month since my baby girl called me to pick her up, and I cherish every moment spent with my daughter since. I didn't even realize it, but there's been an easiness around Erin that definitely hasn't been there lately.

Thanksgiving has come and gone as we dive into December. Erin and I picked out a tree last weekend and decorated the house. While I've loved the extra time with Erin, it's startling that I miss Melanie as well.

Izzy stayed longer than expected, not hitting the road until after Thanksgiving last week. It did Melanie some good, but it meant she spent her free time with Izzy and not me. Now that Izzy has left and things are calm as nothing has happened at Melanie's house since the fire, I itch to see her.

Enough so that I leave work on my lunch break, hoping to spend time with her for a few minutes on her day off. I curse when I pull into my driveway. Once again, she's balancing on the tips of her toes on top of her fucking stepladder in a pair of tight leggings, hanging lights. Her shirt has risen, exposing a sliver of skin on her lower back. Between that and her fine ass in those black leggings, my dick tries to distract me from the true issue here.

Christmas music plays from her phone on the porch railing, and as I approach, I hear her softly singing.

"Are you fuckin' kiddin' me, Mel?" I ask once I'm close enough.

She squeaks and, not entirely unexpectedly, she falls. I am prepared and easily catch her.

"Damn it, Austin! Why do you do this to me?"

"Why do you do it to me?" I parrot back. She knows she can borrow my ladder. I even reminded her last week when we were texting and she mentioned her plans to decorate. It doesn't surprise me she's going all out for Christmas, considering she decorated for Halloween *and* Thanksgiving.

"Shouldn't you be at work?" she asks as I carry her inside. "Hey, I'm not finished."

"It's my lunch break. I came to see you," I answer as I sit on her couch and move her so she's straddling me. Then, I surprise us both by admitting what's been on my mind. "I've missed you." I cup her face and press my mouth to hers without hesitation. For entirely too long, I've been thinking of when I'll touch, kiss, and fuck her.

It's been driving me up a wall that I haven't spent a ton of time with her lately. Not sure if it's as simple as that or because I'm bothered, it's bothering me. All I can think about as we kiss as if it's been years and not weeks is that this seems like the best time to reacquaint myself with Melanie.

Melanie must agree because she tugs on my shirt until

it's up and over my head. I make quick work of doing the same to her.

"I'm gonna leave my ladder with you before I leave, and you're gonna use it," I order.

She nods eagerly as if I just offered to have *her* for lunch instead. Our hands are frantic. Our bodies impatient with our hips already rocking against one another.

"How long is your lunch break?" she asks as we shed the last of our clothes and she hovers over me, pausing for my answer.

"I'm the boss, sweetheart. It's as long as I want it to be. Thinkin' it'll be a long one." Unable to wait a second longer, I thrust up just as she crashes down on me. The pure euphoria that comes with being with her again is absolutely fucking crazy. It's almost as if she somehow became embedded beneath my skin. Without her, I'm left with a large, gaping hole.

Ridiculous. Fucking nonsense is what it is.

I shut off all these *emotions* and focus purely on the sensation of fucking Melanie, both of us losing our minds with need and pleasure, because it's been too goddamn long.

Our release comes entirely too soon. I require days with her, not the mere hour I plan to be here. Even now, I can't stop touching her. My hands slowly trail a path nowhere and everywhere. Mel has her head on my shoulder, puffs of her labored breathing hitting my neck.

"Are we still going to The Mad House tonight?" she asks, her voice quiet.

"Not in a sharing mood, to be honest."

"Amelia's birthday is tomorrow, though," she reminds me. Right. We're supposed to go out tonight because

Melanie works tomorrow, and apparently my sister has other secret plans that don't include the rest of us.

I honestly don't know if I can keep my hands off her, even in public. I must have been quiet for too long as Melanie lifts her head to look at me with a little smile.

"You missed me?" she questions.

My hands move to her hips, and I rock her against me. "We gonna talk or are you gonna let me eat?" An eyebrow raises in question at her. I don't want to talk about the fact that I missed her. I don't know why I said it. I don't know why I do. I don't know how I feel about it yet. What I *do* know is that she loves when I go down on her, so that seems like the perfect way to distract her.

Melanie squirms on my lap. She missed me too. It's clear as day in her eyes. Or maybe I'm imagining things. At the very least, she missed this part of being with me.

We spend the next hour trying to rack up a long list of orgasms before Melanie shakes her head.

"I can't do it again. I don't even think I can finish hanging my lights."

When she glares at me, I laugh. "*That* is what you're thinkin' about right now?"

I snag the blanket off the back of the couch and cover us up from where she lies on top of me, both of us completely satiated.

"Well, I mean, other than seeing you later tonight, it was my only goal today."

I shake my head as I laugh at her again. "If you feed me lunch, I'll finish your lights and help you with the rest." The words leave my mouth before I can think anything of it. God, I must be desperate for the extra time with her.

At my offer, Melanie burrows deeper into me and draws lazy circles on my chest over my heart.

"I thought you had to get back to work?"

"Boss, remember?" I take a moment to look around her living room as I realize it looks different. She's gone balls to the wall inside with Christmas decorations as well. "Looks great in here, Mel."

"Thanks. I don't really remember Christmas before my mom left, but I know afterward, my dad made it a big deal. All the holidays, really. My dad always made spending time with family and making sure I knew I was loved a big deal." Her sigh confuses me a bit.

"What's wrong?"

"I haven't talked to them in a little while. I told my brothers off for what happened with Tyler after they assaulted him, and then I found out my dad knew and encouraged them. I just...what was the point, Austin? All it did was piss him off, and they were the only ones who initially got satisfaction from it." She falls silent, and I let her have that, waiting to see if she needs me to speak or not. After a minute, she continues in a soft voice, "I wish they understood that I'm not like her and they don't need to smother me with their love. I'll never leave or turn my back on them like she did."

I don't feel as though anything I say will comfort her, so I give her a squeeze. After a bit, we have lunch, and I shoot my right-hand man at work a text that I'm taking the rest of the day. With ease, Melanie and I spend the next few hours decorating her yard and house. It's almost too much but somehow not. By the time we're finished, there's enough time to shower before we're supposed to meet everyone at the bar.

Melanie and I ride together after I surprisingly had to spend a few minutes trying to convince her there was no need to ride separately. Our crowd is already at a big booth where the seating is in a half-moon. Amelia sits close to the center, Silas next to her, and then my buddies, Dean and Matthew.

Melanie slides in to sit next to Amelia, and I slide in after her, nodding at the guys while Amelia and Melanie hug quickly.

"Happy Birthday, Amelia," I say after Melanie has told her the same.

"Thanks. Where's my present?"

I roll my eyes. "You'll see it soon enough." She's been talking about a pair of rocking chairs for her front porch since she saw a set I did for a client. One of the guys from work should be dropping them off as we speak.

The girls dive into their chit-chat and, naturally, I tune them out and start talking with the guys. At some point, Amelia insists on playing darts. She and Melanie aren't that great, but they have a blast.

"What's really going on with you two?" Silas asks, dragging my attention from Melanie to him.

I may have griped about not seeing Mel to him, and it was a mistake.

"It's nothing." I want to frown in disgust at the unpleasant taste that sentence—that *lie*—leaves in my mouth. This thing with Melanie is way more than that, though I'm not sure I understand exactly what it is. What I do know is that I don't want it to end.

"Has Angela been bothering her?"

"Surprisingly, no. She's been quiet with me, too, and hasn't even asked to see Erin."

Silas grimaces and shakes his head. "Don't let your guard down. Someone keyed Caleb's car and slashed his tires last night."

I curse under my breath. When I asked him why he was

driving his father's car, he mentioned his car being in the shop, but not why. I'm assuming because Erin's listening ears were nearby, but still. He could've texted what happened.

Silas is quiet for only a moment longer. "You like her," he states. "You might want to tell her that. Don't make the mistake of falling into the comfort of being able to fuck her. At some point, she'll want more. Either from you or from someone who will give it to her. You need to decide if you're going to make it so you're the only option she sees—make her fall for *you*—or if you're too much of a coward."

His spiel pisses me off a bit, but I'm quickly distracted.

"Oh my God!" Melanie shrieks. Her arms shoot up in the air, and then she claps and jumps in place for a second before whirling around to face us. "Did you see that?" Before I have a chance to fully react, she hugs me and gives me a loud smack on the lips. "A bullseye!" she squeals before giving me another kiss, this one lasting longer and being deeper.

Immediately, I wish we were back at my house because this afternoon was not nearly enough alone time with her.

"Good job, sweetheart," I murmur, unable to let her go even as her legs drop down to the floor. She looks ridiculously happy, which I don't think I've ever seen. It doesn't help my gutter-filled thoughts either. "We should head out early," I suggest quietly, keeping her flush against me.

Melanie tenses so suddenly that I immediately release her, confused at her one-eighty.

"I'm sorry. I shouldn't have done that. We're supposed to be a secret anyway, right?" She steps a full two feet away from me. I frown as she glances around to see if anyone saw.

"What's the matter, Mel? Really?" I ask softly, taking a step closer to her.

She suddenly looks nervous. With a small sigh, she takes my hand and leads me outside to where it's quiet and we have a bit of privacy.

"I should've told you sooner."

"Told me what?" I grit. I don't like where this is going whatsoever. Any time a woman says she needs to tell me something, it's nothing I enjoy hearing. With that in mind, I brace for whatever Melanie has to say.

Melanie wrings her hands together and takes a deep breath. "Angela has been harassing me. Or she was at least."

"What?" I exclaim. "Since when?"

She winces. "Since right after she saw us. She started with texts and then emails of all things, and she showed up at my job. She has popped up in a few places, actually, and I was about ready to make a police report for harassment, but she's been quiet this past week, so I thought it was over. I'm sorry, Austin. I got carried away in there, and then I was worried that Angela might start up again if she caught sight of us or heard about it."

"Why didn't you tell me?" I ask, unable to keep the anger out of my tone.

"I didn't want you to worry, and it wasn't anything I couldn't handle."

My first thought is just...fuck me. The second is maybe I could use her harassment of Melanie to prove she's also unstable. And the third is that I absolutely hate she's been shouldering this alone.

I take her hand and pull her flush against me. "You should've told me," I tell her softly.

"For you to do what?" she asks curiously.

"To simply know. I can tell Angela to back off. Whatever you want."

"She's already backed off, and our arrangement is still

intact. Maybe she finally believes me since I kept telling her we aren't together."

I frown. Silas, unfortunately, is right. I like Melanie. If it came down to keeping her for myself or letting someone else have her, I'd rather keep her. "What if we were?" I say.

Again, Melanie's body tenses and catches me off guard. "Is that something you want?"

"Do you?" I counter.

She's quiet for a moment before she says, "I didn't think you wanted anything else; I haven't thought about it because of that. I thought..." Her brows pinch together, and she shakes her head. "I haven't given myself permission to want more. Should I?"

I lift a hand to cup her jaw. "I will if you will." Her eyes widen in surprise. "Let's head out. I want you at my place tonight."

Chapter Thirteen

Melanie

Austin does indeed take me to his house. I barely have a chance to slip my shoes off before he drags me to his bedroom. Apparently, we haven't fucked enough today. This is the first time we've had sex in his house—in his bed. It's the first time that it feels like... *more*.

"This is weird."

Austin chuckles. "That's not exactly what a man wants to hear after fucking four times." He runs his nose along my shoulder and inhales when he gets to my neck. "Why is it weird?" he asks softly. Tenderly? Either way, it's said with a tone that makes me melt.

"We're always at my house."

Austin hums. "I love having you in my bed, though. We'll need to do this more often." He flattens his hand on my stomach and then moves it until he's cupping one of my breasts. "Good weird?"

"Yeah," I whisper.

"Gonna let me take you out somewhere?"

I'm still trying to wrap my mind around the fact that

Austin wants more from me. For us. It's hard to believe. I can't stop thinking about the image of him promising he didn't want more and how genuine he seemed. And how he wanted to keep me a secret.

"Are you sure you want to?" I can't help but ask.

Austin nudges me until I'm lying on my back next to him. There's a question in his eyes as if he can't believe I'd ask.

"You said you didn't want a relationship and that you'd keep me a secret from Angela. You've really changed your mind?"

His knuckles drag lightly from my collarbone straight down my sternum, between my breasts, down my stomach, and back up again before he repeats the process. Goosebumps pop up all over my skin. It takes all I have not to shiver in response.

Austin grins like he can read my mind. "For better or worse, I like you a lot and want to know more about you, do more with you, and keep you close. Angela hopefully won't be a problem once I win in court against her. Does it bother you that she might be a colossal pain in our asses? More than she already is, that is."

Angela doesn't trouble me all that much. She's annoying and infuriating, but nothing I can't handle. My relationship is shifting with Austin, though. "I want to be certain you're sure and that the rug won't be pulled out from underneath me at some point."

"I don't change my mind."

I raise an eyebrow at him because he's already changed his mind from not wanting a relationship to wanting one. After a beat, Austin laughs.

"Okay, I'll amend my statement. I don't scare off easily over something I want." My breathing falters for a moment as he drags his knuckles back up until he runs them along my jaw before sinking his fingers into my hair, cradling my head. "I want you," he whispers slowly, packing a punch with each word.

The feeling that Austin, with his simple, straightforward statements, is putting himself out there more than usual causes my heart to beat faster.

"Where do you want to go?"

He grins, and butterflies erupt in my stomach. "We'll figure something out. We should probably get some sleep." He relaxes next to me, pulls me close against him until my arm is over his waist and my head on his shoulder. "Night, sweetheart," he rumbles.

"Night."

When Austin asked what I wanted to do for our little date, I think he was stunned by my answer. I'm actually an easy girl to please. It's the following Friday night. We've been at his place of business for over an hour now. He's been working on a double rocking chair and talking me through everything he's doing.

First though, we ate at none other than Go Ahead and Fry Me. Just the reminder makes me chuckle. The moment Mrs. Millie saw us, she hooted and called out to Mrs. Edna, "I called it, Edna! You owe me a fat hundred!"

I'm not sure how I feel about the old ladies betting on whether we'd get together, but ultimately, I decided it was adorable and went with it. After we ate, Austin drove us over to his business.

I have to say, I love watching Austin work. He's so

passionate about it, too. He explains how he felt lost after he left the military, as did a bunch of his buddies. How, even though they didn't see combat during their deployments, the service still did a number on them. The change to civilian life was tougher than any of them thought it would be. To the point that they eventually followed him here when he started his business in order to remain together and work together. Some apparently work with Silas, who had no interest in joining Austin's company, which is why he joined the police department.

Another part I love is his dedication to the craft. He mentions that he's a novice, constantly learning and evolving his skills. His apprenticeship program started as a way to help others get started as well.

And then there's the physical aspect of his work. He moves through the workshop with ease and confidence. His calloused hands move across the wood almost reverently, and his tone is passionate as he explains the process to me.

Currently, he's working on a two-seater rocking chair. Their rocking chairs, single or double, are some of his most popular, both the ones for exterior and interior uses. He boasts with pride about the fact that his furniture will last for years and can be passed down among the generations of a family.

I watch as Austin hand-sands the wood, smoothing out some of the roughness. My focus is completely on the movement of his body until he laughs and breaks the spell I'm under.

"You look like your mind is in the gutter."

"It's on the way there," I admit, causing him to laugh again. "I'm not interested, though. My body is still on a break."

Austin moves to stand between my legs, completely

abandoning his work. His fingers trail slowly from my knees up. "Are you sure? Maybe you need a little convincing." He waggles his eyebrows, and I laugh.

"I'm positive."

The creak of the door causes us both to turn our heads. His cashier stands there, frozen while she stares at us.

"Hey, what are you doing here?" Austin asks. His tone is casual and surprised.

Her gaze bounces between the two of us before dropping to where Austin's hands still rest on my hips. I swear, something flickers across her face. Something hard and cold that adds to how uneasy she already makes me. But it disappears so fast I wonder if I imagined it all.

"I, uh, I forgot something and came back to get it. I saw the light on in here and decided to check it out."

Austin frowns and faces her fully. "That's not very safe considering we're closed, and you didn't know who is back here. Let me know next time you need to come back in after hours, okay?"

"Right. Will do. I'm gonna go. Sorry to have interrupted." A smile that screams fake to me plasters on her face. "You two enjoy your evening."

She hurries out through the front. Austin turns back to me, picking up the sandpaper and returning to work.

I can't help but ask him about her. "How long has she worked for you?"

"Almost since the beginning. Ever since we picked up enough business that I could put someone up front. She's solid. Kinda quiet and a momma hen. She'll bring everyone lunch and sit back here with us sometimes."

I pick at imaginary lint on my knee and ask, "Have you ever...?"

Austin stops working and glances over at me. "Had sex

with her?" he finishes with surprise in his tone. "No way. You don't cross that line with people you work with. It's never even crossed my mind." He pauses and then asks with a frown, "You trust me, don't you?"

I nod. "Yes, of course. I was curious about her, that is all."

Maybe Austin hasn't thought about her that way, but I wonder if she has. Nothing Austin said makes me think she's always as unpleasant as she was the first time I met her. He knows her better than I do, so maybe I'm over analyzing things unfairly.

Austin eyes me for a moment. He grabs my hips and places me down in front of him, turning me to face his work-piece. "Think it's time you helped."

There's something soothing about his work. The repetitive motions of some things, the attention to detail, and the allure of transforming pieces of wood into functional pieces of furniture. At some point, I wonder if he feels the same watching me partake in something he loves as I did when he helped me bake.

About an hour later, the work all done for now, Austin swivels me and pulls me flush against him. Yes, it totally does the same to him. When he places me on the counter and unbuttons my jeans, I find I'm not as opposed to sex as I thought.

There's always an exception to be made for Austin.

"Daddy!" Erin laughs. "What is that?"

We're decorating cupcakes today at Erin's request. She said the theme was animals, so that's what we've been trying to ice on top. Apparently, she's not impressed with Austin's skills. To be fair, there is a brown heap of icing, and I'm not too sure either what he's doing.

"What? It's a bear!"

I can't help but snort, which makes Erin laugh harder and Austin look at me with mock hurt. It looks like a pile of poop, maybe, but not a bear.

"Where are the ears? And the eyes?" Erin asks.

"I'm working on it, baby girl. Relax, you'll see in just a minute; this will be the best bear you've ever seen."

She hums in response, making me laugh again. My laugh is interrupted by a yawn, the third in the last handful of minutes.

Austin's gaze narrows at me. "You need sleep."

I wave him off, knowing he's likely concerned about me, but my sleep hasn't been as bad as it was. "It's nothing. I haven't been feeling one hundred percent, and work has been crazy. I'll be right as rain in a week or so." I have been more tired than usual, but then again, Austin and I have been fucking like crazy. Good sex makes me sleepy, so it's probably his fault, anyway.

He frowns, but doesn't get a chance to say anything before Erin peers over at my cupcake and mirrors her father's expression. "Is yours a..." She tilts her head. "A cow?"

"Of course it is. It doesn't look like one?"

"No, it does," she reassures with a pat on my shoulder.

"More of a baker than decorator, I guess," Austin tells me with a smirk.

It appears so, since Erin thinks my cupcake isn't up to snuff either. The amazing thing is, she's actually not half bad. I can tell what she's doing at least.

"Your cat looks great," I tell her. Erin beams with pride

in me. She shares how she asked her mom for a cat once, but was told no, and one day she hopes she can get one. Maybe I can convince Austin to let her have one.

It hits me now that if things go *really* well with Austin, Erin could be my stepdaughter. My heart warms both because Austin trusts me with his daughter and because Erin honestly is a great kid. It would be an honor for her to look at me in that way.

Pump the brakes, Melanie. It's entirely too soon to think like that!

I flick my gaze from Erin to Austin. He's watching me with an expression I can't quite decipher. Could I picture us together long-term? See myself as a second mother figure to Erin? Living in this house? Having a little kitten run around?

I mentally shake my head and focus back on making my cow look like a cow. The time for daydreaming about a future with Austin is not now.

Maybe one day.

Chapter Fourteen

Austin

My girl loves Silas more than all of my friends, so when he made a point to call and speak with her, I knew I was in trouble. There's a hockey game this afternoon, and he's inviting the guys—and Erin—over to watch it. Since she adores her Uncle Silas, she all but demanded we go over.

At least it's not too late of a game, so we won't be out past her bedtime. She has school tomorrow after all.

"Silas!" she screams as he opens the front door. He crouches and is ready as she crashes into him.

"Hey, sweet girl. You've grown, what? Six inches since I saw you last? What are you? Ten now?"

She giggles as intended. "No! I'm only seven! And," she frowns, throwing a disapproving look my way, "Daddy hasn't measured me lately, so..."

"We'll make him check," he promises. They continue chatting as he takes her hand and leads her inside.

I have no choice but to follow. My girl sweet-talks all of my buddies, enthralling them with her charm. If I didn't already know I have good friends, I would based on how they entertain my daughter. Even as the game gets underway, they cater to her conversation if she shines her light on them.

At some point during the first period, Silas stands, lifts his chin and tilts his head in an effort to advise me to follow him to the kitchen. I do. He grabs the beers, so I walk to the pantry to grab more snacks.

"I, uh...just wanted to apologize for how I came at you about Melanie."

I shrug. It's not a big deal. Silas probably has the biggest heart of anyone I know, my little girl included, and he has a hard time keeping quiet when he cares. That means he is sometimes butting his nose where it doesn't belong, even if it backfires on him.

Silas sighs. That's not something he normally does, which tells me something weighs on him, more than just what he said to me. "I know what it's like to start one way with a girl and then feel trapped there. I don't want you to make the same mistake, especially considering all she's been through."

I frown. "There's a woman stressing you out, Silas?"

He's a good guy, but he normally keeps it casual. He has some unwarranted demons haunting him. The idea of a relationship both terrifies him and leaves him yearning.

He gathers the beers and a bottle of water for Erin in his hands. Silas faces me, his face carefully blank. "You and Melanie seem to be a nice match. Don't fuck it up by not acting to make it something more, by being stupid and complacent. That was my point, but after that night at The Mad House, I don't think Melanie'll let you go easy." He flashes a fake grin my way. "Oh, and I have it on good authority that Mrs. Herman is looking to retire."

My brows pull together. "Mrs. Herman, who owns Bake My Day? Why are you telling me this?"

Silas shrugs and disappears back into the living room.

I'm still flabbergasted, though, that a woman has gotten under his skin. I can't help but wonder who she is. We'll all find out at some point, I'm sure. And why do I need to know Mrs. Herman is retiring? Thinking of the bakery makes me think of Melanie.

Like how she lights up when baking, or talking about. How it is what she was born to do, but has let others convince her otherwise.

And now we're about to have a vacant bakery.

An idea—a crazy, definitely over-the-top, and too-much-too-soon idea—forms before I can stop it.

Now I know why Silas mentioned it. While I'm sure he didn't have the same idea, his goal is likely the same: to see Melanie with her own bakery. Buying it outright for her will probably send her running to the hills, considering we haven't been dating all that long yet. And I'm not sure she can be convinced yet. Not when her father has been so against the idea.

I shove the idea away altogether and rejoin everyone in the living room. Melanie remains on my mind, though. And for some reason, my stomach is in knots.

The longer we stay at Silas's house, the more uneasy I get. I have this urge to check on Melanie, so I shoot her a text.

AUSTIN

Hey. Work good? Back at home?

MELANIE

Exhausted. Crazy day. Falling into bed now. Talk tomorrow.

My gaze flicks to the clock. She's crashing early. I send her another text to wish her a good night.

Still, as time ticks by, I have this niggling feeling to get away and check on her. I've officially lost my mind. There's no reason to take off to see her. Yet my gut screams at me to do just that.

What excuse would I make anyway? Erin is with me, so it's not like we could stay long. Maybe she'll wake up later and I can sneak her over. The urge to have her with me turns uneasy at some point, even once I'm home.

I shove that feeling down and focus on my responsibilities for the night. Getting Erin a bath. Getting her ready for the night by reading her a story, making sure she brushes her teeth, and helping her pick out an outfit for tomorrow.

Later, I'm in bed only ten minutes before I groan and pop back up. If I see a light on, I'll text her. If I don't, I'll suck it up and go to sleep myself. My footsteps are soft as I make my way to the living room. The closer I get to the window to peer out, the worse I feel. Something isn't right.

I'm proven correct when I notice an orange glow illuminating from outside and then I look out to see Melanie's house engulfed in flames. Fuck, is she still inside?

Without hesitation, I run over to her house. Thank God, I grabbed my phone when I left my room. I call in the emergency, advising of the fire and her address while shouting her name in case she made it out. Panic quickly consumes me.

I don't fucking see her!

My heart batters against my chest at the thought of her being inside. The front of her home is lit with flames. There's no way to barge in safely. I run around toward the side of the house where I know Melanie's room is, not that it'll do me any good. She's on the second floor.

I round the corner and my heart stalls as I watch her fall with a scream and crash to the ground. Christ, she jumped out of the window.

"Melanie!"

She attempts to groan, but it dissolves into a fit of coughs. I kneel next to her and immediately pick her up. A small shriek escapes her.

"My ankle," she sputters.

I glance down to see her foot hanging at an odd angle. Carefully and as fast as I can, I carry her over to my place, placing her gently into a rocking chair on my front porch.

Melanie stares over at the massive inferno that was her home. Sirens wail in the distance, getting closer and closer.

"Are you okay? Anything hurt?"

"My house," she whispers.

"Sweetheart, I know, but I'm more worried about *you* at the moment. What else hurts?"

Melanie falls silent. Tears stream down her face, still unable to look away from the flames. Within minutes, fire-fighters are doing their thing, and paramedics place Melanie on a stretcher. I push my way through to grab her hand gently.

"I'll meet you at the hospital, okay?"

She nods before pulling her hand out of mine as the first responders request I step out of the way. I don't wait to see her off. I rush back inside, change my clothes, and then lift Erin out of bed.

"Daddy?"

"Just rest, baby girl. We're going on a little trip to Daddy Caleb's."

By the time I walk back outside, the blaze doesn't seem any smaller, and the ambulance is gone. Erin falls asleep within a minute of being in the car. I call Caleb to give him a heads up I need to drop Erin off. I'd take her to the emergency room with me if I had to, but I'm not sure what kind of state Melanie will be in or how long we'll be there. Ultimately, the best place for her is with Caleb.

After I do that, I finally make it to the hospital and am let back to wait for Melanie, who is off getting x-rays done. While I wait, I call Silas as my mind thinks about what happens after she gets discharged.

"I've heard," Silas answers after two rings. Of fucking course the gossip has made its way around. He's not even on shift today. "What do you need?"

"Can you swing by and get Amelia? Go to the store and buy some essentials for Melanie. All she has is literally the clothes she was wearing."

"Sure. No problem. She gonna stay with you?"

I pause. Apparently, that was all the opening Silas needed to butt in *again*.

"Her family will bulldoze the poor girl and overwhelm her. I just want to know if you're gonna give her a safe place to land and be there for her or if you're gonna allow her family to swallow her whole." He pauses, surely for dramatic effect, and then adds, "Or maybe I need to step in again."

My jaw clenches. I remember the last time he stepped up because I was staying within the role we set for ourselves.

"Austin?"

"I fucking hear you. Just get my sister and have her grab some stuff. I need to find out if anyone's called her family yet."

Before he can spout more of what he believes is wisdom,

I hang up. I stand ready to pace when they roll Melanie back into the room. They have already put her ankle in a cast.

Before I can take my place next to her bedside once she's situated, her father barges in.

"Melanie! Thank goodness you're okay. How are you feeling?"

Her eyes well with tears, but she doesn't try to speak.

He cups her face and kisses her forehead. "It's okay. You're okay," he reassures. "Charlie and Warren are already on their way. As soon as you're discharged, I'll take you home. You can stay with me until this gets resolved."

Every word he speaks causes Melanie's shoulders to slump more and more. It pisses me off that even in a moment of need, because of how they treat her, she doesn't want to lean on them. She probably does somewhat, but at the same time, knows what it'll bring if she does.

"Actually," I interrupt since he's yet to acknowledge me. "Melanie said she wanted to crash at my place. I already have my sister bringing some things for her, too."

Melanie looks relieved, while her father appears outraged.

"Why is the neighbor boy here?" he asks, ignoring me.

"I found her," I answer anyway. To her, I pointblank ask, "Did you change your mind about coming home with me?"

We haven't discussed it, but it gives her an out if she wants it.

"Of course she did. She'd rather be with family." He pats her hand, which he holds. "Your brothers and I will look after you."

Melanie flicks her gaze between me and her father. It

148

seems clear to me she'd rather stay with me, but maybe part of her doesn't want to, especially since it's next to her destroyed house.

"Charlie and Warren don't need to come," Melanie starts. "I'll stay with you, but I'd like to stay with Austin tonight."

Her father frowns. "Why would you want to stay with the neighbor boy?"

Neighbor boy, really? I certainly understand the thought of disliking the man after your daughter—as I dread the day Erin starts dating— but there's no need to be flat-out disrespectful to me.

"I'm her boyfriend," I snap. Technically, we only had the one date, but still. That garners me his full attention as Melanie stares at me in disbelief.

Before anyone can say more, her brothers burst into her room and immediately crowd her. They envelop her in a hug, and it's then Melanie truly breaks down, crying on their shoulders from where they sit on either side of her.

With a quiet sigh, I step out into the hallway and lean against the wall. I've never felt so useless in my life. I can't believe I'm envious of her stupid fucking brothers. All because she's letting them hold her while she cries. I stand up straight when her father joins me.

He eyes me for a moment before he orders, "Give me a quick rundown on who you are."

"Austin Lowe. Originally from South Carolina. Served four years in the Marine Corps, during which I knocked up my then-fiancée. Afterward, I moved here so I could be near my seven-year-old daughter. I own Chair Necessities and have been seeing your daughter since shortly after she broke up with her douchebag of an ex."

That's all he's getting from me right now. I don't care for the man much as it is at this point.

He surprises me by sticking his hand out, which I shake. "Mr. Fields. It's nice to meet you officially, Austin. You must give my daughter a lot of comfort as this is the second time she's ever chosen to stay with someone else over me. I'm assuming you're the reason she didn't come to stay after the break-ins and vandalism?"

I nod in confirmation.

"See you continue to be that kind of person for her."

He pats my shoulder before stepping back into Melanie's room. I'm not sure how long I stand out there, giving her space and privacy with her family, before Silas and Amelia round the corner.

"How is she?" Amelia asks.

"As good as expected. You can go in and see her."

She doesn't wait and rushes in to see Melanie.

"What are you doing out here?" Silas asks, handing me the bags of items they picked up for her.

"Giving her a bit of time with her family. And before you open that big mouth of yours, she's coming home with me tonight, and we've been on a date, so back off."

Silas grins. "I knew you weren't stupid. You guys need anything else?"

"No. Have you heard any news about the fire?" I keep thinking about what might have caused it. Was it her Christmas tree? Only a real tree would do for Mel, and those can be fire hazards.

"They put it out, but her house is a total loss." He takes a breath, never once looking away from me as he says, "Buddy of mine said they're thinking arson. I'd keep that to yourself for tonight at least."

Fuck, fuck, fuck. Someone did this on purpose?

Someone tried to *kill* Melanie. Burn her alive in an excruciating manner.

Panic sears through me, and I can't help but burst back into her room. I need to see her. The idea of possibly losing her has terror coursing through my veins.

Chapter Fifteen

Melanie

The ride to Austin's is quiet. I feel both full-blown sadness and anxiety about seeing what might be left of my home, and I also feel a little concerned about Austin. He raced back into my room earlier, looking terrified. He said he was okay, but he forced his way through my visitors until he was next to me with my palm in his.

Even now, his hand tightly clutches mine.

The sight of my house steals my breath. Well, the ashes and charred remains. There's nothing left to salvage. The fire ruined everything. All because I forgot to set my alarm and lock my door when I came home.

My car sits out front, untouched, but my keys were inside the house. Christmas is soon, and I have *nothing*. Nothing but what's in the bag at my feet and my car. The weight of the loss renders me incapable of taking a full breath. All I can do is cry and hyperventilate as I stare at the ruins.

Suddenly, Austin blocks my line of sight.

"Austin," I sob. "My house."

"I know, sweetheart. I know. I'm so sorry." He unbuckles me, lifts me, and tells me to grab my crutches for him. I bury my face in his neck as he carries me inside and to his room. He leaves me long enough to change and then crawls in next to me. Still, the tears fall.

His face nuzzles my nape from where he lies behind me. "I'm so glad you're okay," he whispers. His fingertips trail a path from my shoulder down my arm, leaving goose-bumps in his wake. "We'll make things okay again," he promises. "I'll stay home with you tomorrow."

"Thank you." I carefully roll over, wanting to be face-to-face with him. Or at least, have the ability to press my face into his chest. I don't know how to even begin to absorb what's happened. The devastation is too great. "Make me forget; just for a little while," I quietly beg.

Austin doesn't respond. Not verbally, at least. Instead, he touches, kisses, and moves through me with such passion wrapped in tenderness, gentleness, and reverence. It's almost too much. Overwhelming. We've never been together like this. There's still heat, but it's not a frenzy. It's not rushed.

It's shiver-inducing as he kisses me slowly and thoroughly. It's breath-stealing as he thrusts into me with a level of control I didn't know he possessed. It's heart-melting as his hands glide over my body as if I'm a precious treasure he doesn't want to lose.

Afterward, Austin wraps me up in his arms, kisses my forehead, and I crash from the day's events.

Austin and I spend most of the day together, curled up on his couch. It's hard to sit idly, but what exactly am I supposed to do? I'm out of work for two months. I have zero possessions other than my car, which I luckily realized my father has a spare key for, so I can use that at least. Talking to the insurance company *again* was a blast as well.

His front door suddenly opens, causing him to extract from me and stand.

"Daddy! Miss Melanie's house is—" Erin stops herself short when she sees me. "Miss Melanie!" she cries out. She runs over and jumps up onto the couch next to me. "Are you okay? Your house is gone!"

I swallow hard, hoping the tears will stay away. "I know. I'm okay. Just hurt my ankle." Broke it, but still. "I'm happy to see you, though. Want to bake some lemon bars?"

"Mel," Austin starts as Erin shouts, "Yes!" over him.

"Sounds like a plan then. I already sent your dad to the store earlier, so we have all we need. Do you mind grabbing my crutches?"

She does, and we head for the kitchen, leaving Austin to talk to Caleb. Baking is exactly what will soothe my aching soul. I was banking on Austin being unable to say no to the both of us. I sit in a nearby chair with my leg propped while Erin does most of the heavy lifting for me, anyway.

Once Caleb leaves, Austin enters the kitchen with a glare my way. There's literally nothing to be upset over. I'm sitting and taking care of myself just fine. Austin helps Erin press the crust we made into the pan. We work on the topping next, not really discussing much outside of the next steps or measurement of ingredients.

Once we're able to add the topping and place everything back in the oven, Erin abandons us to play in her room.

"After you take it out of the oven, you'll dust powdered sugar on top. My brother will be here in a second to take me over to my dad's. Thanks for letting me stay here."

"Are you sure you want to go?"

I'm not, but I can't stay here. Amelia is an option, but for some reason, my gut says I should stay with my father. With that, I nod in answer to Austin's question. A knock sounds on the door. A quick glance confirms it should be my brother since we discussed yesterday what time he would pick me up.

"Time for me to go."

Austin looks as if he doesn't want me to leave, but he doesn't say anything other than to call if I need him once I get my new phone. After a quick kiss on my forehead, I'm off.

I start to second-guess myself, when on the way to my dad's, even Charlie asks, "Sure you want to stay with Dad? You can always stay with me or Warren."

I assure him that I'll be fine. However, when we pull into Dad's driveway, Charlie tenses. There's an unfamiliar car parked next to Dad's, so maybe that's why?

"Ah, why don't you stay with me?" Charlie puts his car in reverse, but I reach over and grab his hand.

"No. Dad's is fine." I unlock and open my door before he can object. Once my crutches are situated, I head to the front door with my brother following behind me with much anxiety as he continues to suggest we leave. "What is your deal?" I ask as I push the door open.

The first sound that hits me is a woman's laughter. I follow the sound to the kitchen, not thinking much of it. What I find makes me stop short. There's a woman wrapped in my dad's embrace as he apparently peppers kisses on her neck.

Charlie clears his throat. Dad lifts his head and then places at least three feet between him and the woman, who turns towards us. My eyes widen.

"Ms. Ketner?"

She smiles softly, with a bit of embarrassment. "Hi, Melanie. It's nice to see you again."

I can't do much other than stare. Why is one of my eighth-grade teachers in the kitchen getting kissed by my dad? Clearly, they are together. Is it new, and that's why Dad didn't tell me? But wait, Charlie knew.

"She's your girlfriend?" I ask, needing confirmation.

"No," Dad answers while Ms. Ketner replies, "Yes."

My brows raise. "Since when?" I ask Ms. Ketner since Dad seems unwilling to tell the truth.

At this, her cheeks turn pink. "Started the summer after you were in eighth grade."

I rear back. They've been together for all these years? Over ten years? Looking over at Charlie, I ask, "Did you know about this?"

He nods. "After they had been together for two years."

An overwhelming sense of betrayal washes over me. Why wouldn't they tell me? What about this equates to everyone knowing but me?

"I'll be in the car." It's not graceful, but I begin to turn and make my way out of the house.

"Melanie, wait!" Dad shouts.

"No!" I yell back without looking. The most important thing is leaving. "You've all lied to me! And for no reason!" I can't help myself and slowly pivot to face my father, who looks stricken at the turn of events. "If you're happy, Dad, I'm thrilled for you. You deserve happiness after what happened with Mom. But under no circumstances do I deserve for you to lie to me for *years* and make my brothers lie to me, too!" He opens his mouth, but I snap, "I don't want to hear it! I'm staying with Charlie."

Dad lets me leave without another word. It takes a few minutes after I've situated myself in Charlie's car before he appears. The ride to his house is silent while I stew. If yesterday hadn't taken everything from me, and Christmas wasn't so close, maybe I wouldn't be so distraught. But that did happen, and my emotions are raw.

Once at my brother's, I plop myself onto his couch. Pure exhaustion weighs on every fiber of my being. Charlie brings me a bottle of water and sits next to me.

"How could y'all not tell me?" I ask quietly, anger simmering within me so steadily, I'm surprised I'm not raging. "Y'all treat me as if I'm incompetent and can't do anything without your approval or review. I struggle with feeling helpless because of how y'all treat me. I feel so suffocated by the three of you, but I put up with it because I love y'all and I *know* if I called, no matter when or what you're doing, you'd drop everything to come help me. So I don't understand why you'd keep something like this from me."

Charlie shocks and confuses me with his response. "What do you remember about Mom?"

"Not much. We lived with her some, and then one day, she dropped us off with Dad and left. Why?"

He sighs and turns toward me. "For the record, we told Dad he should tell you. You've been a point of contention between him and Pamela because she wants more, but he refuses to tell you."

I shudder at him calling her Pamela. She's still Ms. Ketner to me. "But why?"

"After you were born and before the divorce, Mom changed. She used to just up and leave with you. For days, or weeks, or even months sometimes, she would take off

157

with you and drop off the face of the earth. Dad wouldn't know where you were, if you were safe, or when you were coming back.

"She would eventually return, apologize profusely, and things would be fine for a bit. Then, while Dad was waiting for the divorce to be finalized, she left with you." Charlie takes a deep breath. "You were gone for a year, Mel. She shows up one day, drops you off, and then disappears. We never saw her again."

My brows furrow together. "I thought you and Warren were with me the last time?" What I thought was the only time.

He shakes his head and lowers his voice. "You have no idea what Dad was like that year you were gone. The money he spent trying to find you. It was hell, Melanie. So when he got you back, when he had his precious little girl in his arms again—"

"He became overprotective."

Charlie nods. "And you were devastated that Mom was gone. You refused to speak for three months, and it took another three before you warmed up to us and settled. That wrecked all of us. Dad wasn't sure how you'd react to Pamela, so he refused to tell you in case it would upset you."

Well, at least I understand my dad and brothers more. The sting of betrayal fades away. The anger fades only to be replaced by understanding, hurt, and emotional exhaustion.

Part of me actually wants to see my dad now. Charlie pulls me into a hug. Whatever tension remained leaves me. The comfort of my brother wraps around me; it's nearly as good as if Dad were here instead.

"Still mad?"

I take some time to mull over my response before I answer him. "I'm hurt. I understand why Dad did what he did. But Charlie, you all lied to me for over a decade. Was it easy? Easier than telling me the truth? And avoiding that all for what? Y'all think I'll be like Mom and leave? You've all made me feel like I can't do anything alone, and now, on top of that, I find out you've been keeping this massive secret. Why do y'all think I'll be like her and walk away?"

"That's not true." His wince tells me otherwise.

"Isn't it?" My voice cracks. "The hovering, taking over, not wanting me to bake. It's all because of Mom. You're all terrified I'll end up like her."

His silence deflates me further. It's confirmation that I'm right, and the hurt only grows.

Tears I didn't think I had in me fall. "I'm not her, Charlie. Maybe we have things in common, but that doesn't mean I would ever abandon the people I love. None of you trusted and believed in me enough to know that. You took the hurt she left and placed it on me, whether you meant to or not." I shake my head.

Charlie looks remorseful. "We've tried convincing Dad to tell you, but the fear of losing you never went away for any of us. I'm sorry we made you feel that way. I'll talk to Dad and Warren and we'll work on it, okay?"

"Thank you." This right here is why I can't hold a grudge against them. If I had spoken up sooner, I wouldn't have had to endure for as long as I have, but I didn't want to upset them either. And if I had spoken up sooner, I'd know why they truly feel the way they do. My family spent a year not knowing if I was alive, dead, harmed, unharmed, nothing. I'm still hurt, but understanding his reasons goes a long way.

Charlie's phone rings in his pocket, causing us to break our embrace. Of course, it's Dad.

"He's gonna want to talk to you," Charlie warns before

he answers once I nod. Knowing the real backstory, I don't want to ignore him when he's probably afraid all over again. It takes only but about thirty seconds before Charlie hands the phone to me.

"Melanie—"

"I'm not mad you're with her, Dad. I was upset you kept it a secret when everyone else knew. I'll come back over tomorrow, and we can talk. Maybe you should grovel to Ms. Ketner and invite her to dinner tomorrow." It'll take me some time before I can call her Pamela.

Dad exhales heavily. "You're not upset with me anymore?" The relief is almost palpable through the phone.

"No, I promise. You were worried for nothing. I'm happy for you. Honest."

"Oh, Melanie Rose, I'm so relieved and thrilled to hear that. I'll go grovel now, and I'll pick you up from Charlie's tomorrow, so we can replace your phone."

"Sounds good, Dad."

We exchange love yous and then hang up. I don't waste much time after that before I head to bed. It's been an exhausting, emotional rollercoaster of a few days, and everything seems to slam into me. I need to sleep. Tomorrow will be a better day.

Dad shows up at Charlie's by noon the next day with lunch. We sit around Charlie's table and after a few minutes of awkwardness, Dad breaks the silence.

"I'm so sorry I kept Pamela from you. Charlie said he told you a little about what happened with your mom. I didn't realize you didn't remember that. God knows I haven't been able to forget it."

At that, I reach over and squeeze his hand, earning a wobbly smile.

"And I'm sorry I put my trauma on you. Your mother did a number on all of us, and we didn't mean to put that on your shoulders."

He shakes his head and falls silent. I can almost feel the unspoken words, so I stay quiet too, waiting.

"You know she loved to bake, but what you probably didn't know is that she'd bake for days before she would disappear sometimes. She was always baking, but it was different when she was able to take off. The kitchen would be spotless. There would be a theme, like everything chocolate, or everything has nuts. It was like she needed to leave something behind because she knew she was taking what mattered most.

"Later when we were separated, I didn't have the baking to clue me in that she was ready to hightail it out of town. And then, the year she took you—" His voice breaks right along with my heart when two tears shamelessly fall. "I didn't know if I'd ever see you again, Melanie Rose. It was the worst year of my life. Once I got you back, I swore I'd never do anything that might drive you away."

I reach over and grab his hand. "Dad, I would never do that. I love you, Charlie, and Warren too much. I need y'all to trust that I can handle my own life, though."

"I know; Charlie mentioned that too. We've never thought you couldn't do it. It was us trying to make sure you needed us."

"I'll always need y'all, Dad."

He smiles, stands, and pulls me up for a hug. "I love you so much, Melanie."

"I love you too, Daddy."

Later, we leave to run a few errands. There's shopping for basics I need and picking up a new phone.

"What are you smiling about over there?" Dad asks as we head home and I fiddle with my phone.

I haven't had a chance to check in with Austin, but it's apparent he's been thinking of me as text messages started filtering in as soon as it was activated.

"Just catching up on some texts," I reply as I read them over again.

AUSTIN

Have you gotten a new phone yet? I miss you.

Gonna need you to call when you do.

The lemon bars were delicious, by the way. Erin wants to try something else new this weekend, if you want to come over.

Maybe you can spend the night.

Hope everything is okay with staying at your dad's. Amelia is always an option. Or me.

When you get a chance, send me all your favorite baking supplies and equipment.

The texts stopped about an hour ago. I glance up as Dad slows down because of an accident. First responders are already on the scene. My gaze catches sight of the vehicle, which looks like Angela's, and then I see some of my co-workers help Erin out of the car.

"Dad! Stop! Pull over and stop."

He does, asking me what's going on, but I ignore him as I hurry as fast as I can out of the car. What in the world is

Erin doing with Angela? My understanding is she isn't to have Erin unsupervised.

I hobble across the street until I get to where Erin is.

"Erin, honey, are you okay?"

Tears fall rapidly down her face. "Miss Melanie," she wails. I grab her hand as she's already on a stretcher.

"It's okay. Are you hurt?"

She shakes her head. "Momma is, I think."

"Let's just get you checked out, alright?"

"Are you staying with me?"

"Yeah, I won't leave you until you're back with your dad. Let Roger look you over, okay?"

She nods, and I hear my father say, "Melanie, what's going on?"

I turn to him. "I don't know, but this is Erin, Austin's daughter. I'm riding with her to the hospital, and I need to call Austin. I'll call you later; you can head on home."

"I'll follow you there," he says instead.

At this point, they've loaded Erin onto the ambulance. I glance over where Angela's car rests in the ditch. It looks like they are still working on getting her out.

"Melanie?" I turn at the sound of Roger's voice. "You coming? They are sending another bus for the driver."

He doesn't need to say more. It takes a bit to get into the back of the bus with my injury, but I'm not leaving Erin alone. Once I'm situated, Erin still cries, but swears she's okay. Roger gives me a look and then continues to check her vitals. He casually mentions that she wasn't buckled in as he questions her about any pain. Considering the car was upside down, it's a miracle she doesn't appear to be hurt.

"I'm going to call your daddy, okay?"

She nods, so I do.

Austin answers immediately, but sounds frantic.

"Sweetheart, I'm happy you're calling, but I can't talk to you right now. Somehow the school let Erin leave with Angela and I've got no fucking clue where she is. I'm waiting for the police to arrive, so we can report this."

"Austin, she's with me."

"Why the fuck does she *do* this to me?" he continues as if he didn't hear me. "I swear, if she runs with my daughter, I'll—"

"Austin," I interrupt louder. "Erin is with me."

There's a long silence and then in a careful tone, "What did you just say?"

"Angela wrecked her car, and I came upon the scene with my dad. I'm in the back of an ambulance on the way to the hospital with Erin. She seems to be okay. Do you want to talk to her?"

"Yes; I'm heading your way now."

I hand the phone to Erin, and she talks to Austin until we arrive at the hospital and someone takes us into a room. He bursts into her room and gently pulls her into a hug, which only makes the poor kid cry harder.

It takes about fifteen minutes before she's settled enough that the doctor can check her over again. Because of taking precautions, they soon cart her off for some scans with Austin accompanying her.

Dad manages to make his way into her room. "Is she okay?"

"Seems to be, but running some tests to be sure."

"I'll wait with you until they come back." He sits down in the chair next to me and takes my hand.

Erin'll be okay. I feel it in my bones.

Chapter Sixteen

Austin

My nerves don't settle until it's confirmed Erin is okay. The absolute terror that coursed through me when I went to pick her up only to find out that Angela had was a feeling I never want to experience again. Apparently, Angela provided falsified documentation that made it seem as if the previous order was now null and void, which is why the school let her take Erin.

Currently, the officer questions Erin to understand what happened after that.

Erin sends a nervous look Melanie's way at the question of what occurred in the car. Melanie gives her a reassuring smile, which spurs Erin to share.

"Well, she was upset and talking a lot. She said she was mad at Daddy for taking me away and that he let Miss Melanie come over. She said we were going far away, just the two of us. She got mad when I said I didn't want to go. I don't remember everything she said." Erin doesn't say much more than that.

Once Erin is fully discharged, Melanie and her father, who has waited with her, stand to leave.

Melanie goes to speak, but I beat her to it. "You're coming home with us. We'll swing by to get your things, but you're staying with us tonight." There is an inexplicable need to have her there, and I'm not in the mood to fight it.

"I have plans," she says with zero conviction and a quick glance at her dad.

"We can reschedule the dinner," he tells her. "Sounds like it may do you all some good to spend some time together."

After a moment, she tells me, "I already have my bag in the car."

"Great. Let's go."

After stopping to grab takeout, we arrive at my house and take our places on the couch to eat with one of Erin's favorite movies playing.

My phone vibrates with a text, so I check it.

SILAS

She's been charged with DUI, kidnapping and child endangerment, to name a few. Just wanted to update you.

Y'all need anything?

AUSTIN

We're good. Thanks.

I turn my phone off and toss it onto the coffee table. All I need right now is to sit here with Erin and Melanie. I'm half tempted to have us all sleep in my room tonight too. The idea of either of them being out of my sight sours my stomach. I already plan to keep Erin home from school tomorrow and, obviously, also stay home from work.

After setting Erin up with the shower, she saves me the

trouble of ordering her to my bed by asking if she can stay in my room tonight. It doesn't take us long until we're settled in my bed. Me in the middle with Erin on one side and Melanie on the other.

All we need is a good night's sleep, and then we'll start tomorrow with trying like hell to forget the past two days ever happened.

"Daddy?"

"Yeah, baby girl?"

She's been quiet most of the evening, and I haven't wanted to question her too much. She's been through enough today.

"Will Mom be okay?"

I take a breath in hopes it steadies me. Angela is stable but still hospitalized with her injuries. Silas confirmed she's facing serious charges that could lead to jail time. How do I explain any of that other Erin?

"She'll be okay. The doctors are still taking care of her."

There's a stretch of silence before she asks another question. "Do I have to see her again?" Her breath catches. "She said we were going so far away that I'd never see you again. I don't want to move away from you ever."

I tighten my arm around her and kiss the top of her head. "Don't worry about that, okay? You're staying right here with me."

"Okay, Daddy." She burrows closer and within minutes, she's relaxed and asleep next to me.

Melanie squeezes my other hand, and I whisper an order for her to get some sleep too.

Lying there with the two people who matter most to me in the world, all I can think is how no one will ever take either of them from me.

Both Erin and Melanie have been pretty quiet today. Unsurprisingly, Erin is sore as the aftermath of being tossed around inside the car hits her. We've been lazy in the living room, watching movies. Caleb came over to check on Erin; she's currently resting against him now.

There's a knock on my door. I get up and, after checking the peephole, open the door with a bit of confusion.

"Stacey? What are you doing here?" *Shouldn't you be at work?* I think.

She beams a smile at me. "I tried texting earlier, but didn't get a response. I wanted to stop by, see if you need anything."

"We're good, but thanks. Taking care of the front office will help plenty."

Her smile falters a little, but she nods. "Okay, I'll get back to it. Glad Erin is okay." She pauses. "It must've been terrify—"

"I really don't want to talk about it right now. I appreciate you checking in, but it's not necessary. I need to get back to Erin and Melanie." She's being kind, and I realize I shouldn't be so curt, but my nerves are still frayed from yesterday. I don't want her here.

She frowns and asks, "Melanie's here?" Before I can respond, she seems to catch herself. She beams a smile at me. "You're in good hands then. I'll let you get back to them. I'll let the guys know everyone is good and just text if you need anything."

I nod, and thankfully, she steps away and walks to her car. Once I've closed the door, I walk back over to the couch, kiss the top of Erin's head, and say, "Baby girl,

Melanie and I are going to sit out back for a little bit, okay?"

"Okay, Daddy," she replies without looking away from the screen.

I help Melanie stand and then follow her outside where I take a seat on a rocking chair and then pull Melanie to sit in my lap, being mindful of her ankle.

I rest my chin on her shoulder and ask, "Absorbing things okay?"

"Like how someone tried to kill me?" The investigators stopped by today and shared that tidbit with her. "Like how my house and all my things are gone?" She glances at me and says, "My dad has had a girlfriend for years and didn't tell me; I was supposed to have dinner with them last night."

"A bit overwhelmed then," I surmise, making her crack a smile.

"Yeah. Trying not to think about it, honestly. You doing okay?"

"Much better now that she's home and Angela gets to stew behind bars. Personally, I hope she stays there, but I'm not happy at all for Erin. I dread telling her what's about to happen. The only good to come of this is Erin's officially all mine."

Despite Angela scaring the shit out of her yesterday, Angela is still her mom, and this is going to hurt her.

"Maybe you should stay here instead," I say. Her father is stopping by soon to pick her up. I can explain things to Erin. I still don't want her too far away.

"Don't want to let me go?"

"No," I reply honestly.

"I need to," she replies quietly. "But I'm sure my dad won't mind waiting a little longer."

I smile, but before I can kiss her, Caleb slides my back door open and pokes his head out.

"There are some people here for you."

"I'm not expecting anyone," I say as I help Melanie stand.

"Not for you. Melanie."

"Me?" Melanie questions with confusion. We walk inside to find the owners of everyone's favorite diner, placing bags on the table and ordering Caleb outside to grab more. "Mrs. Edna? Mrs. Millie? What are you doing here?"

The women converge on Melanie in order to pull her into a hug. "Oh, dear, we're terribly sorry to hear about your house and that it took so long for us to come by," Mrs. Millie explains.

"I don't understand."

"We figured there are a lot of things you need, so we collected donations," Mrs. Edna adds. She hands Melanie a thick envelope that appears to be stuffed full of cash. "And Lenny said one of his houses just became vacant, so if you want to rent it, it's yours. He was rambling on about the first three months' payments being on him if you baked him some more of those lemon bars."

"And should you need help with anything at all, you let us know," Mrs. Millie orders. "Here's our numbers and Lenny's as well as the address to his rental. You can even call us if you need a ride somewhere and your go-to folks aren't able to take you. Whatever you need, reach out and we'll take care of for you."

A sob rips out of Melanie, likely overwhelmed by the show of kindness. The women pull her from me, and I snag her crutches before they fall to the ground as they hug one another.

"It's okay, dear. We'll help get you through this. This

town loves you, and we're happy to be here for you," Mrs. Millie tells her.

"It's too much," Melanie half-heartedly protests.

"Nonsense," Ms. Edna says with a wave of her hand. "Take care of her, Austin." The women help balance Melanie as I step forward to let her lean on me instead. They then converge on my daughter to check on her after her ordeal as well.

"I can't believe they did this."

I can. Melanie sucked me in for a reason, and it's because she's a fantastic person.

Things seem to return to normal over the next week. I'm back to work, Erin is back to school, and Melanie remains at my house for now. What isn't normal about my week is that Bake My Day has been on my mind. It doesn't help that I drive by it on the way to work.

At some point, I am still in my truck, parked out front, and stare at the storefront. I'm only out front for five minutes when my phone vibrates with a text.

SILAS

Finally making your move? Or still thinking about it like a chicken?

AUSTIN

What move? What am I supposedly thinking about?

SILAS

Bake My Day. You're parked outside and have stopped by three times this week. I have eyes and ears everywhere.

I curse, toss my phone in the cup holder, and pull out of the parking spot. Instead of forgetting about the crazy idea, I call my sister.

"Hey, big brother. What's up? My niece still doing okay?"

"She's fine. I have a question."

"Shoot."

"Hypothetically—"

"Oh God."

My hand tightens on the steering wheel. "Be serious for a second. Hypothetically, if I bought Melanie a bakery, would that be romantic or a complete overstep?"

The line is silent for so long, I wonder if she's hung up until she nearly screeches in my ear.

"You want to *buy her a bakery*?"

"Yeah. Mrs. Herman is retiring soon according to Silas. We both know Melanie was born to do this. This would be perfect timing since she's out of work. I want to give this to her."

"Austin." Amelia's voice is careful. "That's a huge offering. Do you have the funds for that? Why not take the idea to Melanie to see if she even wants to do it herself?"

I had thought of that. "Because I'm selfish and want to give it to her." A small part of me wonders if she would protest about the timing or funds, or even her father. She may jump at the opportunity, or she may wish to delay it. But I spoke true. I want to be the one to give this to Melanie. "I want to give it to her and tell her it's because I believe in her so much. That she can do it. That she'll be amazing. And then stand back and watch her do just that."

Amelia's voice is soft, but pride. "Then that's what you should tell her when you give it to her. She'll be ecstatic."

With my sister's seal of approval, I make one pit stop on

the way home to see Melanie's father and get his too. Even though things have improved between them, something tells me she'll want the reassurance.

The next day, I walk into Bake My Day as Mrs. Herman enters from the back.

"How may I help you today?"

"I heard you were thinking of retiring."

At this, she props her hands on her hips. "Who's been yapping about my business?"

"Is it true?" I ask instead of answering her.

"Why do you want to know?" She eyes me as if I'm about to rob her instead of asking simple questions.

We're going to keep asking questions, I guess. "Do you know Melanie Fields?"

Mrs. Herman scoffs. "Do I know her? Do I *know her*? Of course I know her!" She wags a finger at me as if she needs to give me a stern talking to. "That girl keeps trying to put me out of business. She gives away her baked goods, and then, because people don't want to ask her for more, they come asking me if I can give them whatever she baked for them. That girl is something else."

After a brief pause, her features soften and she says, "I heard what happened to her. She doing okay?"

I nod. "She's healing."

Mrs. Herman grabs the kitchen towel off her shoulder and wrings it in her hands as she narrows her eyes at me. "What're you here for?"

"I want to buy this for her." I motion around the bakery.

The towel falls to the floor. She stares at me for a long moment. "You what?"

"She's my girlfriend and, as you've pointed out in a roundabout way, baking is her calling. So, I want to buy the business from you. You can retire, and she can start living her dream."

"You're serious," she states.

"As a heart attack," I confirm.

Mrs. Herman whistles. "If she doesn't love you yet, she will. Let me think about it. I was only planning on closing and leasing the space to someone else. I hadn't thought about selling the whole kit and caboodle. Let me ponder it and leave your number. I'll give you a call when I'm ready."

That's all I can ask. I give her my number, and when she asks if I'm buying anything, I decide it might be in my best interest to do so. I leave with two bags full of goodies.

When I pick Erin up from school, she spots the bags immediately. "Ooh, what did you get? You know, I enjoy baking, but sometimes it's nice not to have to bake myself when I want something sweet."

I laugh and reach back to hand her one of the bags. Considering she always has a sweet tooth, I imagine she'd like someone else to bake for her quite often.

"Well, I thought we all deserved a little treat today."

"A little? You must've wiped her out!"

Nearly.

"Daddy?" Erin asks after being quiet for a few minutes, and no doubt devouring a croissant.

"Yeah, baby girl?"

"Will Miss Melanie have a good Christmas at her daddy's house? She *loves* the holidays. Is his house decorated good enough for her?"

These are all great questions. Before I can answer, Erin says one more thing.

"Maybe we should check out her daddy's house, and if it looks even a *little* grinchy, we should ask her to stay with us. I'm sure Santa can still find her since it's next door to where she used to live."

"What if she thinks *our* house is a little grinchy?" Erin gasps, and I add, "Melanie goes all out for the holidays. You remember how she decorated for Halloween and Thanksgiving. And I promise, her house was more decorated than ours is."

Erin thinks about this for a moment. "Let's go shopping then! We can add more things for her."

"What if she wants to stay with her family for Christmas?"

Another pause. "Well, she'll visit us, won't she?" There's hope in her voice and maybe a little fear that she's wrong.

"I'm sure she will, baby girl."

"Then we have to make our house better! Turn here and go to the store, Daddy."

I laugh and obey her commands. Anything to make my place more appealing for Melanie is good with me. Not to mention that I'm sure it's hard for her to be without a home during a holiday season, even if things are slowly improving between her and her family.

Erin wants to ensure our house is full of the Christmas spirit. She quickly fills the cart until I begin to wonder where in the world we're going to put all of this when we get home.

"We have plenty; let's go and start putting this stuff up."

"Wait! We need that!" She points at something. I groan internally when I realize what she's pointing at. She wants a second tree. This one has fake snow and multi-colored lights. My instinct is to say no, but Melanie would love it if I had multiple trees up. I'm pretty sure she had three—one in the living room, kitchen, and bedroom.

"Please, Daddy? Miss Melanie will love it; I know she will!"

Fuck me.

Chapter Seventeen

Melanie

About an hour ago, I answered the phone, expecting Austin, only to find it was actually Erin on the other end. She said they had a surprise and asked if I'd come over for a movie night. It was clear she hadn't asked Austin first because I heard him in the background, asking who she was talking to.

He ended up assuring me he was still on board with her plans. Since Warren was visiting Dad, who has moved Ms. Ketner in, he offered to drive me over. Charlie kept his word and talked to Warren and Dad. They slip sometimes, but it's been amazing to see how they don't overdo it with me already.

"We love you, you know. You've always been very capable," Warren says on the drive over. "We only want to make your life easier by doing things for you. And I realize now that we didn't exactly use the right words to convey that. I'm sorry."

"Thanks." His words mean more now that I know they all mean it. "Do you...do you think Dad would be okay if I became a baker?" It's been on my mind ever since my injury. It's not that I'm dreading returning to work, but since everything has happened, I feel as if I can seek their support in ways I couldn't before.

Warren's hand tightens on the steering wheel. Anything related to Mom is still unpleasant for both of my brothers.

"I love it," I tell him quietly. "And I'm only thinking about it."

"If it'll make you happier, then go for it. We will support you. Maybe just let Charlie and me know first so we can give Dad a heads up."

As soon as he parks, I partly launch myself over to hug him. "Thank you!"

"Yeah. Yeah." Warren lifts his chin toward Austin's house. "You like him?"

"Oh, my God." I roll my eyes. "Yes, and let's leave it at that. Thanks for bringing me. I love you."

"Love you too, sis."

I wave off his help to get inside and make my way to Austin's front door, which opens as I reach the porch.

"Miss Melanie! We have a surprise for you!"

"I know; you told me." My voice fades as I step into the house. "Wow." I don't even know where to look. Christmas covers every inch, *and* he has a second tree.

"Do you like it? It is Christmasy enough for you?" Erin asks, bouncing on her toes.

My gaze lands on Austin, who leans against a nearby wall with a soft smile. I glance down at Erin. "It's perfect. You two did all of this for me?"

"Yes! Will you spend Christmas with us?"

"Hey, we agreed not to ask her that. I told you she may want to spend it with her family," Austin chastises, stepping into the conversation.

"I want you to spend it with us, though," Erin tells me, completely undeterred. As if she is worried she won't be convincing enough, she adds in a pout.

There's no way I can say no. "I'd be honored."

Erin squeals. She goes to grab my hand and pull me further into the house, but remembers my crutches and steps back. She talks a mile a minute now, telling me about the snacks they have ready and the stack of movies she wants us to watch.

Austin tells her to get some of the snacks while he comes over and takes my bag from me.

"Are you sure, sweetheart?" he asks quietly. "Don't let her force you to stay."

"I mean what I said. I'd be honored."

The same smile his daughter gave me appears on his face. "You've made us both very happy."

Somehow, I don't think it's as happy as they've made me.

It's a new year, and I'm officially in my new home after spending an amazing Christmas with Austin and Erin. I'm still emotional over the idea that my perfect little town gave me this. This is more than I could've even dreamed of. My home was stolen from me so irrevocably, and sweet Lenny provided me a place to call mine until I'm back on my feet. It means more than I would've thought.

I get my own space and don't have to crash at my dad's, or my brothers', or even at Austin's. The rental is a cute little two-bedroom home. I've been here a week with someone in my family stopping by every day, and Austin stops by after work, too.

I've been ridiculously tired, but also busy, which is good. Just as I was on the verge of going stir crazy, Austin dropped off an assortment of baking items. My dad brought over groceries, and I've been baking up a storm ever since. There's no way I can let the folks in this town be as nice to me as they have and not bake something in return.

I've been baking up all kinds of things. Lenny sets them out at his hardware store, and folks drop by to snag the goodies. I'm all baked out right now, though, and I really want to see Austin.

My dad gives me a lift and drops me off at Austin's work. I've had dinner with him and Ms. Ketner a few times now, and I'm super thrilled for my dad. After seeing them together, I hate that I'm the reason he didn't move on with his life sooner. They are moving full steam ahead now, though, considering she has moved in with him and he's proposed.

Right now, I need to see Austin. I manage to make my way inside, and Stacey glares at me.

"Can I help you?"

"Just heading to the back to see Austin."

She cuts me off, surprising me by blocking the way. "You can't just waltz back there."

"I can't see my boyfriend?" I ask incredulously. Her eyes flare. "Do I need to call him again?"

She narrows her gaze and steps out of the way. I walk past into the employees-only area and into the back, where it opens up into a warehouse. Men work at their various workstations. I don't see Austin, so I head to his office.

"Yeah, we could do that. Can you drop it off next week or do you need us to pick it up for you?" Austin smiles and lifts a finger. "Perfect. See you then," he says before tossing his phone onto his desk. "What a pleasant surprise. Lock the door and come here, sweetheart."

A shiver runs through me at his order. As I turn the lock, Austin moves some things off his desk. As soon as I'm close enough, he takes my crutches to lean them against the wall and lifts me onto his desk.

"Good day?" he asks, bending and placing kisses along my neck down to my shoulder.

"Yeah. I've missed you and thought I'd stop by."

"So happy you did. Erin is with Caleb this weekend. I want you with me at my place." He gropes me all over, it seems, and my body sings, begs for him.

"What if I don't want to wait?" I cup him through his jeans.

He grunts. He doesn't hesitate or double-check if I'm sure. He lifts my dress and steals my panties, pocketing them. His mouth crashes into mine while his fingers dip between my legs.

"Don't make a noise," he warns me. "I don't need my men hearing you."

I can stay quiet as long as he doesn't stop. Austin and I have somehow gotten even closer in the past month or so. We haven't been together long, but we're getting to the point where I don't know what my life was like before him. Where I don't want to imagine life without him.

"I love you," I whisper.

Austin freezes. "Don't fuck with me, sweetheart. Are you just saying that because..." His fingers wiggle.

I laugh and slap his shoulder. "No. God, way to ruin the moment, Austin. I'm over here being vulnerable with you and sharing how—"

His mouth crashes against mine. "Love you too, sweetheart. Let me give you an idea of how much."

And boy, does he.

A week or so later, I'm in my home, asleep, when my eyes suddenly fly open, as if I've heard a noise. My ears strain while I blink rapidly as if that'll help me adjust to the darkness. My breath catches. I *did* hear something.

Footsteps. Slow, steady, and light.

Panic almost consumes me immediately. Someone is in my house. Shit! Fuck! Damn! What am I supposed to do? I'm a freaking sitting duck! There's nowhere for me to go.

I reach over, grab my phone, and dial for help. The footsteps get closer, but then a different sound, as if whoever is pacing. As carefully and quietly as I can, I drag myself toward the closet; it's my only option.

"Hello? What's your emergency?"

"My name is Melanie Fields. 456 Seventh St. Someone is in the house," I whisper.

"And where do you think you're going?"

I freeze as surprise filters through me. It's a woman. I was so close to making it to the closet. Slowly, I turn around, unable to stop myself from blurting out, "Stacey?"

"You! You ruined everything!" she screeches, waving her hands and causing me to realize she has a gun. Her eyes dart about, unfocused. Dark circles rest beneath them as if she's been awake for days. Her hair is a mess. Both dirty and haphazard, like she's been running her hands through it or tugging on it.

Terror courses through me so strongly that I don't

realize I start muttering over and over, "Oh, God. I'm going to die."

"You should've died in that fire," she spits. "I won't take a risk like that again. The nerve you have!"

She...she's the one who tried to kill me? At this point, we were thinking it was Angela, honestly. The police questioned her, but she hadn't admitted it. Now I know why. She was innocent.

"Why are you upset with me?"

"Upset?" She cackles humorlessly. "I'm *furious*. I've been working with Austin for three years, and I was finally close to having him ask me out. I was so close!" she screams. "And you ruined it! The fucking nerve you have to fuck him in his office. I'll get you out of the picture, and then he'll finally see me." Her finger squeezes the trigger, and I scream as the bullet hits my leg.

I'm still stuck on the fact that it's his cashier. "You've broken into my home, vandalized my things, and burned my house down because you have a crush on Austin?" I ask incredulously.

"Only the fires were me. His stupid ex is the one who broke in. She's dating Tyler and convinced him to help her."

I can't comprehend this right now. I lean against the wall, struggling to stand even with my crutches under my arms. This is crazy, and my leg fucking *hurts*.

Stella lifts her arms again and levels the gun at me. "I'm finishing this one way or another. I'll make sure you die this time."

Blue lights filter into my room. Finally, she hesitates.

"Want to kill me badly enough to go to jail over it?" I grit my teeth as dizziness swarms my head. "Willing to see if Austin wants a damn thing to do with you after you kill me?

Do you think you'll get away with this? You don't have to do this."

With bated breath, I wait to see if this is how it ends.

"You don't have to do this," I repeat, pleading with her.

Just when I think she's decided not to end my life, her hands steady, and she says, "Yes, I do."

Chapter Eighteen

Austin

My phone rings nonstop and wakes me up. I answer the call from Silas and demand, "What the fuck do you want? It's late and—"

"Melanie's been shot."

"What?" I sit up and rub my face. "What did you say?"

"Stacey. Stacey shot her."

The absurdity of his words gives me whiplash. "Stacey shot Melanie," I repeat slowly, the statement sinking in. They don't make sense. Stacey? My employee? Shot Melanie? The woman who is the love of my life?

"Get your ass to the hospital, Austin," Silas snaps. "That's all I know right now."

If terror didn't begin to fill me, if the unknown of Melanie's condition didn't twist angry knots in my stomach, I'd comment on how he's like a town gossip. He always finds shit out and is always one of the first to know. To be fair, his job helps.

"Amelia's on her way to stay with Erin. Get dressed and go. If I happen to hear anything else, I'll call. Otherwise, I'll meet you there. I'm calling her folks." Softening his voice, Silas adds, "She'll be okay, Austin. Just get to the hospital."

I disconnect the call and rush to dress. By the time I grab my keys, there's a knock on my door. I unlock it and yank it open. Amelia throws her arms around me in a quick hug. She pulls back and wipes her tears away.

"Go. Let me know when you have news."

She doesn't have to tell me twice. I rush out to my truck and then speed like a bat out of hell to the hospital. Fucking despise this place. We've been here too often in the last month.

Once at the emergency room, I rush inside and demand an update.

"What's your relation to the patient?" the nurse asks, entirely too calm in comparison.

"Her boyfriend. Please, is she okay?"

"Sir, unfortunately we can only release details to the family and—"

"You can't be serious!" I shout, unable to stop myself.

A hand grabs my shoulder, and a look shows her father. He gives my shoulder a quick squeeze. "I'm her father. What can you tell me about my daughter?"

"She's in surgery; she was shot in the leg and chest. They had to insert a chest tube on scene for a collapsed lung. That's all I know at this point. Please have a seat; someone will be with you as soon as we have an update."

I stagger backward. My damsel is hurt, and there's not a fucking thing I can do. I can't even see her.

"C'mon, son. Let's take a seat."

It's then that I notice Pamela is with him. Melanie and I have spent time with her dad and his girlfriend since right before Christmas. They moved in together after Melanie finally found out about their relationship, and they plan to get married. I like Pamela so far. Not that it matters if I do, but she reigns Mr. Fields in when he gets overbearing with Melanie.

My ass is in the seat for maybe five seconds when Silas rushes in. He comes over and takes the other chair next to me, slapping my back. I give him the update before he can ask.

"Do you know what happened?" If anyone does at this point, it's him.

"Stacey's the one who set the fires, and the operator heard her say Angela was dating Tyler and is the one who did the first break-in. Apparently, she's been vying for your attention for years and was pissed Melanie got in the way." He pauses for a moment, but I don't have it in me to react. Worry over Melanie consumes my mind. "Stacey faced off with the first officers on scene; she lost."

My head falls forward into my hands as it hits me. All of this? All the terror and pain and fear Melanie has had to endure? It's because of me. I had no clue Stacey was truly interested in me. She's been extra friendly lately in a way that I wasn't fond of, but never in all my years would I have thought this would be the result of not indulging her. I would never cross that line. I may hire my buddies to work with me, but I served with most of them. I'm not about to fuck someone I work with every day.

Although it has only been hours, it seems like days pass before someone steps out and calls for the Fields family. We all stand as the doctor comes over to us.

"She's stable and should have a full recovery. We'll keep her for a few days of observation and run a few more tests just to make sure she and the baby are okay."

I don't know if it's relief or surprise, but I fall back into my seat.

"Baby? Melanie is pregnant?" her father asks with a glance at me.

The doctor clears her throat and nods. "Eight or nine weeks by the look of things."

She and the baby are okay.

Holy shit. She's pregnant.

I stand again. "Can I see her?"

"She's on her way to a room, and it may be a bit before she wakes up, but yes. There's no harm in one or two people going into her room. Once she's settled, I'll have a nurse come get you."

Unable to sit, I pace while we wait. There's a baby. A baby! I don't understand how it happened. I mean, of course I do, but it's not like we were trying for this. Did she suspect? Did she already know? It doesn't really matter. I just need to see her.

Nothing could've prepared me for the sight of Melanie in a hospital bed, wearing oxygen, with a chest tube still in place, bandages over her leg, and her poor ankle remaining in a cast. She takes her time waking up. The moment she does, she squeezes my hand, and I hear a wheeze as she tries to talk.

"Just rest," I say. "You're okay." I kiss her forehead and squeeze her hand in return. "We'll talk later. Get some sleep, alright? I'm right here, and your dad is here too." He's actually asleep in the reclining chair. "You're safe, so sleep."

A few tears leak out, and I carefully wipe them away. Her eyelids already flutter. I stay in her line of sight until she closes her eyes. I sit down and take a breath.

She's okay.

Four days after the incident, Tyler is arrested for his part in vandalizing and breaking into Melanie's house, and Angela has a few more charges pending as well. Once they are interrogated, it doesn't take long for them each to confess, though they placed the blame on each other.

The best news, however, is that Melanie is home with me. She'll need someone to help care for her, and I laid down the law that she would stay with me. No one objected, which is good. Erin was worried sick when she heard Melanie was hurt again; she's been staying with Caleb and will be home tomorrow. I wanted Melanie to have at least a day to settle in.

Plus, she still doesn't know she's pregnant. No one wanted to inadvertently stress her out while in the hospital considering we're certain she isn't aware. It's definitely time she knows, though.

We're sitting on my couch, my back against an armrest with my legs stretched out. Melanie is in front of me, leaning back against my chest. It wasn't easy to get into this position, but it was the best one for me to touch her as much as possible.

Melanie has been fairly quiet, but she's been wiped as well. Trailing my fingers down her arm, I ask, "Comfortable? How are you feeling?"

"I'm fine," she breathes. "Thank you for everything."

"I'm always here for whatever you need." I kiss the top of her shoulder. "There's something I need to tell you, sweetheart." Melanie tenses, and I hate it. "It's not bad. At least, I don't think so, but it's a surprise."

"Just tell me, Austin."

"When they were running all their tests," I take a deep breath, "it showed you're pregnant."

Melanie goes to jerk upright, but groans immediately in pain and falls back on me. "I'm what?" she sputters.

"Relax, Mel. Everything is fine."

"Say it again. I don't think I heard you correctly."

With my hands running up and down her arms to soothe her, I repeat, "You're pregnant. Eight or nine weeks, apparently."

"Pregnant?" she whispers. "We're having a baby?"

"Yeah, sweetheart," I confirm just as quietly.

"I don't...I don't think I can wrap my mind around that right now."

"That's fine. I wanted to go ahead and tell you."

She's quiet for a little bit before she says, "I'm sorry you keep having to take care of me, Austin. You're always there to pick me back up and put me together again. Always ready to lend a helping hand. I'm sorry about that, but I greatly appreciate it."

"I don't mind. I'd rather it were me than anyone else. I'd rather it were *you* than anyone else. I'll always be here for you."

I don't think it's hit either of us how our lives are about to change with this surprise. I'm a little more prepared than Melanie since I've been through this before, but still. My and Erin's lives will change. There're all kinds of things to figure out, too.

Melanie chuckles a little, bringing my attention back to her.

"What's so funny?"

"Nothing. Truly. I just didn't realize I was with a man who could drive women to commit crimes for him." She laughs harder at the apparent hilarity before wincing and groaning in pain again.

I don't find her comment humorous at all, and I say as much. It's good she can find humor in the situation, I guess. As gently as possible, I wrap my arms around her. Our biggest focus today is rest and lots of snuggling, so I can reassure both of us we're together and we'll be okay.

Melanie has healed well from her injuries. She's been staying with me, mostly because she finds a reason to stay longer. That's okay. I plan to ask her to officially move in anyway as one part of my Valentine's Day plans.

Erin has adjusted like a champ to the changes, and she's excited to have her favorite baker living with us. We haven't told her about the baby yet, only because we're being extra cautious after everything that's happened. Angela has called her a few times from jail, but we had to end that because Angela couldn't be an adult and talk to Erin about things appropriately. If Angela wants to talk to her, she writes a letter, which I censor if needed. Erin thrives, and it never gets old having my baby girl here all the time. Caleb gets her every other weekend, and Erin seems happier about seeing him regularly again.

Right now, Melanie and I are at the doctor's office to check in on the baby. The technician moves the wand over Melanie's stomach. In less than a minute, the soft whooshing sound of the baby's heartbeat fills the room. Melanie's head falls back, two tears falling.

"There's really a baby in there."

I laugh. "Yeah, sweetheart. We knew that."

"I was paranoid today would be the day we found out it was all a dream or something."

"Not a dream," the technician, Amy, says. "Baby is still in there and looking perfect. I'll print off some photos for you."

The rest of the appointment goes smoothly, and once we're in my truck and leaving, Melanie inhales a big breath.

"I guess we finally need to talk about what's next."

"You move in with me," I answer simply. "Officially. Since you practically are already."

"Are you sure?" Her voice is soft and uncertain.

As soon as it's safe and I find a good place, I pull over. Melanie glances at me as I angle toward her a bit. "Why would you ask me that?"

"You didn't even want a relationship a few months ago, Austin. And now we're having a baby and you're asking me to move in. Are you sure?"

"Of course I'm sure." I reach over and cup her cheek. "Sweetheart, can't you see how much I love you? I'm sorry I didn't say it more often before, but I told you once that you're worth me leaving my past behind and dealing with all the bullshit in the world. Everything is worth it when I get to be with you. So yes, I'm sure. I want you, our baby, and both of you living with Erin and me."

Melanie unbuckles and moves until she wiggles her way into my lap. "I'll move in," she confirms before pressing her mouth to mine. We kiss for a while before I pull away.

"Alright, sweetheart. I know you aren't comfortable, and we still have a few surprises in store, so hop back into your seat and buckle up so we can get on with it."

"There's more?" she asks as she does as I've asked.

"Yeah, a lot more."

Melanie sends pictures of the ultrasound and updates to her dad. We haven't told anyone who wasn't there in the waiting room both due to Melanie's privacy and because once she found out, she was worried something might happen, so she wanted to keep it quiet until she hit twelve weeks.

We'll tell her brothers and Amelia next week once I invite everyone over.

"What are we doing here?" Melanie asks when I park in front of Bake My Day. "Picking up some Valentine's treats? So here for that."

"Yeah, we'll do that. C'mon."

Once inside, Melanie realizes something is off. The place is empty other than equipment.

"Austin? That you?" Mrs. Herman calls from the back.

"Yes, ma'am," I answer. "Be right with you." Melanie frowns as her brows pull together. Before she can ask, I explain. "Mrs. Herman is retiring. She officially retired last week, actually. I meant to bring you up here last month, but then everything happened and it didn't seem like the right time."

I spread my arms out, motioning all around us. "This is yours if you want it, Mel. Just say yes, and we'll go back there to sign the paperwork." Her jaw nearly drops to the floor. I'm certain I've hooked her already, though she hasn't said yes yet. She's looking over this place as if she's envisioning what it would look like if it were hers. "This is your chance, sweetheart. To do what you've always wanted to do. Mrs. Herman will sell us the business, and you can take over. It's yours because I know without a shadow of a doubt that you can take this on and be crazy successful."

Her eyes water as she turns back to me. "You're buying this for me?"

I nod. "It's my gift to you." I step forward and cup her face. "You deserve this, Melanie. And before you worry about your dad, I already talked to him. He said to tell you to go for it if this is what you want."

She cries, but she throws her arms around me. "Thank you, Austin. Thank you so much. I loved you before, but this? This is amazing!" She smacks a kiss onto my lips and grins. "I'm going to have a bakery!" she squeals, causing me to laugh.

"Then get on back here and sign these papers!" Mrs. Herman shouts from the back.

Melanie doesn't delay. She takes my hand and walks into Mrs. Herman's office. I'm two for two so far today. I might as well be on cloud nine right now. Already, I love this life we're building together.

Chapter Nineteen

Melanie

"You'll be great," Mrs. Herman says once Bake My Day is officially mine, and I give her a hug. "Did you tell her what I said when you asked if I knew her?" Austin shakes his head. "I told him that, of course, I knew you. You're the woman giving the baked goods away for *free* and nearly running me out of business on a regular basis!

"I cannot tell you how many times someone would come in here to rave about something you baked for them and to ask if I happened to also sell that dessert because they didn't want to ask you for more."

She gives my shoulder a squeeze. "You have the gift, Melanie, and I'm excited to see you thrive. I'm here if you have questions or want to get my thoughts on anything."

I had no idea she even knew who I was. I didn't shop here often considering I love to bake myself so much. To know the town would ask her about the things I baked for them? It only serves to reassure me further that this is the path I should be on. This is most definitely the right choice.

Mrs. Herman hands over the keys, takes one last look at the place, and then she's gone. I turn to face Austin.

"I can't believe you did this for me. You probably don't want to hear me say this, but I don't know how I can ever repay what you've done for me with this."

Austin wraps me in his arms. "You can repay me simply by letting me see you being happy doing what you love. And of course, bring home any leftovers every day."

At that, I laugh. "You got it." He begins to lead me toward the front of the shop. "Oh, there's so much to do and think about. Menu, prices, grand opening. When am I going to find the time for this?"

"Well, you need to put your notice in at work." My eyes bulge, and he squeezes my hand. "You already know you aren't returning to work, so let them know. I can take care of you while you prepare to open. That's also how you can repay me." I open my mouth, and he cuts in again. "And don't ask me if I'm sure. I am."

"Okay," I squeak and then gasp as something draws my gaze outside. "Oh, my God! Look! It's snowing! We should get going."

A thin white layer of snow already covers the ground. Big fluffy flakes fall steadily. Austin doesn't protest. He leads me to his truck, and we carefully drive back home. It's still weird to see the now-vacant lot next door. The insurance money paid off my mortgage as I have no plans to rebuild; that was that.

"Do you miss it?" Austin asks quietly upon noticing what has my attention.

"Not really. I have a new home that feels like a sanctuary. I think the most disturbing part still is that someone took that from me. Twice." I take a deep breath and glance over at him. "But that's over."

"And we have much better things coming our way."

I smile. That we do. With that thought, I leave my old house behind and walk into my new one. I search until I find a thicker coat, a beanie, and gloves.

"What are you doing?" Austin asks as I make a mug of hot chocolate. "Is it that chilly in here to you?"

"I'm going outside. It's snowing! I love the snow. I want to enjoy it."

"Mel—"

"I can sit in the cold, Austin. So, are you coming with me or not?" I ask, turning to face him with my mug now in hand.

He sighs but nods. I grin and move past him. Within minutes, we've both settled in his double rocking chair. It is something he gave me for Christmas as an almost replacement for the porch swing like I had at my house; it's actually the one we kinda worked on together. Austin moves me until I sit sideways in his lap and his arms wrap around me.

"Think it'll stick?" I ask. He hums in confirmation. "It's so pretty, isn't it?"

"Seen prettier things, but yeah, sweetheart. It's pretty." He doesn't even give me a chance to respond to his sweet comment before he asks, "Do you still want to go out to dinner tonight?"

I love the snow, but I know my limitations. Driving—or riding—in the snow is not on my to-do list ever. When it snows in the south, there's only one thing to do: stay home.

"I'm sure we can find something to do here."

His hands have already slipped beneath my shirt as he kisses my temple. "Tell me again. You said it so casually and easily earlier. And with too many other words. Say you love me again."

I hum and take a sip of my hot chocolate. He's right

197

that it's not the first time, but for some reason, we haven't said it frequently to one another. Still, I can't help but tease him. "Should I? Seems kinda weird with you asking me."

"Melanie." There's a bit of a rumble in his voice, and I shiver as a smile lifts my lips.

"What?"

"Don't play with me." He takes my mug and forces me to look at him. "Say it," he orders. It reminds me of that first night at The Mad House with him. My body obeyed without thought or hesitation.

My mouth does the same today. "I love you. Now and always. I'm glad that of all the people I could've moved next to, it was you. And that you were pushy and unnecessarily concerned over me when I was decorating."

"Unnecessarily?" he repeats incredulously, making me laugh. "It was completely founded. Doesn't matter now anyway because being together means you can stand around and order me to do your dirty work. Can't trust you to do it yourself still."

He shouldn't. Granted, I'll be more careful for the foreseeable future with a baby to consider, but all bets are off after that.

"Do you think Erin will be excited about the baby? And me living here for good?"

"Yeah, sweetheart. She'll be thrilled about the baby. I already asked her if you could stay. She's excited. She's even baking you a cake while she's at Caleb's to officially welcome you home."

"I love her too, you know."

"I know. Can't miss that. We love you too. It's hard not to."

What a crazy life I've found myself in. Done admiring

the snow, I stand, taking Austin's hand, and lead him back inside to get a head start on our Valentine's Day festivities.

"Daddy, did you ask her? Did she say yes?" Erin asks as softly as a seven-year-old can.

Austin places the dessert she made on the table.

"I did," I answer for him. Erin whirls around and screams with excitement.

"Yay! I made you a cake to celebrate. Do you want a slice? Daddy, get a knife and cut the cake."

"You sure are getting bossy," he comments as he does what she ordered him.

"Sorry, Daddy. I get bossy when I'm excited."

We laugh at her antics and within a minute, we're sitting at the table, enjoying her cake. I don't miss the chance to compliment her either. Erin is mostly quiet, appearing lost in thought.

Until she isn't.

"Daddy," she starts almost carefully. "If I got to call Daddy Caleb Daddy Caleb because he lived with Mommy, does that mean I can call her Mommy Melanie?"

My eyes widen to the size of saucers. Austin looks between us for a moment.

"That's not really why you call him Daddy Caleb. Your mom and Caleb were married, too."

"Are you going to marry Miss Melanie then?"

At this, my brows rise, but I also stifle a laugh. Somehow, Austin manages not to let his emotions show on his face.

"Maybe," he admits.

"So I can call her that, right?" She pivots to face me. "You don't mind, do you?"

"Oh, um." I glance at Austin. I don't want to overstep at all and honestly was not expecting this. He shrugs, so I say, "You can call me whatever you want, honey."

Erin beams and runs off to play, leaving Austin and me alone at the table.

"You okay?"

I nod. "I'm surprised and honored more than anything. I didn't expect her to want that, especially so soon."

"Kids are simple and resilient. With all the changes for her lately, I think she's also looking for stability wherever she can find it." He takes my hand in his. "You make her feel safe, Mel."

Erin has impacted my life in many ways, and more and more each day she seems to let me in. Asking me to bake with her. Or what I think about a certain movie or outfit. It's been amazing to spend so much time with her and to see how Austin is with her.

"I love her," I quietly admit. "I would do anything for her."

His expression turns tender. "She loves you too. You'll be a great stepmom to her and a great mom to our baby; you already are." Austin stands and rounds the table as my breath catches at his words. He hooks a finger under my chin, lifts, and gives me a soft kiss. "I love you."

"I love you too." I love them both, and I can't wait until next weekend when we tell Erin she'll be a big sister. All the missing pieces of my life—pieces I didn't even realize were missing—are falling into place, and I absolutely love it.

Epilogue

Melanie

Three Months Later

"Melanie! You're pregnant, for God's sake."

With perfect timing, I fall backward and right into his arms.

"Why do you do this to me? And why the hell are you smiling?"

I may have climbed onto a stepladder when I saw Austin coming. "Because while you make me fall, you always make sure to catch me. Besides, that was staged for old time's sake."

Austin finds no humor in my antics as he sets me on my feet. "You're pregnant," he repeats. "Try not to give me a heart attack."

"I'll do my best," I tell him, holding in a laugh.

"Are you ready?"

Absolutely not, which is why I was distracting myself by torturing Austin. "No. What if I should've taken more time to decide on my menu and prices and decor and—"

"Come on." Austin takes my hand and pulls me to the front.

My breath catches as I spot some people standing outside, waiting to get in. Oh, wait. It's just my family, Erin, Amelia, Silas, and the rest of Austin's friends. Still, Austin leads me outside. I lose my breath again. There's an actual line. A long one. One so long I can't even see the end of it. It looks like the whole town showed up for me. Yet another reason to love Cardinal Point.

"You'll do great, sweetheart. We all have faith in you and are here to support you."

Overwhelmed, I throw my arms around his shoulders. "Thank you for making this happen."

"Not me, Mel. This was you. Now, how about you officially open?"

I turn to the crowd, feeling as if I should say something. Austin gives my shoulders a squeeze as everyone starts to settle and focus on me. It's then that I notice someone standing behind Silas.

Unable to contain my excitement, I scream and rush forward. I throw my arms around Izzy and hug her tight.

"I can't believe you're here!"

"Did you really think I'd miss your big day? What kind of best friend would I be?"

I pull back and ask the most important question. "Are you home for good?"

Her breathing is shaky, but she nods. "Maybe. I think so."

Officially the best day ever. I get to open my very own bakery, and my best friend is moving back to Cardinal Point.

"Go," she urges. "Today is about you."

I return to Austin's side and face the crowd again. With a deep breath, I address them.

"I have no words to express how grateful I already am to each of you who have shown up to support me. Thank you so much for coming today. I hope you like the refreshed Bake My Day." I pull on the door, step inside, and tug the string to turn on the Open sign.

It's time to live my dream, doing what I love every day and being with the best man I could've asked for.

Austin

Melanie has re-stocked the display case three times, and she's officially sold out. The bell rings and in comes one more customer.

"Don't tell me by waiting so you can serve the best last I missed out on all the goods!" Lenny admonishes. "I mean, I knew you would do well, but I'll need to submit a formal complaint," he says with a laugh.

"Mr. Lenny, I thought I might see you today, so I saved a box of lemon bars just for you. Let me grab it."

Melanie disappears into the back and returns a moment later with his goodies. After some back and forth over her trying to give it to him without payment and him insisting, he finally leaves a twenty in the tip jar without technically paying for them.

"I'll take them on the house, but only because you told me you'd think about dating one of my sons, and you moved on to this guy without ever giving them a second thought."

"Sorry. Austin kind of snuck up on me and insisted I pay attention to him," she says, glancing at me with a smile.

"Oh, it's alright. You're probably too good for them, anyway." He slaps the counter as she laughs, thanks her for his bars, and is on his way.

I follow him, locking the door behind him and turning off the sign.

"You did good, sweetheart. Let's clean up quick so we can get you home and prop those feet up."

Melanie sits on a stool behind the counter, a hand resting on her stomach. "Can you believe it? All those people! We sold out! I know it won't be like that every day, but still. It's an amazing turnout."

"It is. I told you that you'd be great at this. How are you feeling?" I ask since she's making no move for us to clean.

"Wore out. Elated. Grateful."

She grabs my waist and pulls me closer, tilting her head up. I kiss her as silently requested.

"Thank you so much for being my little cheerleader and having so much faith in me."

"Anytime, sweetheart."

I let her be while I move to the back to start cleaning. What cracks me up is I told Melanie if she broke up with Tyler, I was certain she'd be happy with someone else in six months. When I said that, I didn't think I'd be the other person, but I'm damn happy I am. I've got the girl, my daughter, and soon another baby.

Life is unbelievably good.

Next in the Cardinal Point series

Up next is Izzy and Eric in *Make Me Whole*. Enjoy the below excerpt where Eric and Izzy finally meet in person. **This is unedited and subject to change.**

My leg bounces as I sit in the chair at the conference table across from Anthony McRae, owner of McRae of Sunshine Homes. He seems nice enough, but this is a big deal. I really want this job.

"Ah, there he is. Kate, this is my son, Eric."

My heart stills. I only know one Eric, but there could be plenty in this town, I guess. Could this be *my* Eric? I stand and turn, the sight of him steals my breath.

Mr. McRae snaps me out of it as he says, "Son, this is Kate Stone."

"Kate." His voice is soft and deep, a shiver tickling down my spine as it caresses my first name.

My heart, which was already beating a bazillion miles a

second, somehow pounds faster in my chest. I somehow manage to keep my eyes open and hold in a sigh.

One word. That's all he's said and god, his voice is perfect. It's not even the name my Eric knows me by, and still, my knees are weak.

"Nice to meet you."

I shake his outstretched hand and manage to repeat the phrase. Eric walks around the table to take the seat next to his father. I sit and smooth out invisible wrinkles in my purple maxi dress.

Please don't let me embarrass myself.

"Eric is sitting in because quite frankly, this is his idea. Word of mouth has been our bread and butter since we opened. We've only had the bare basics when it comes to online presence because we're doing just fine without it, but my son here thinks it's well past time that we grow even more and increase our online presence. That's where you could come in."

I keep my gaze on Mr. McRae, even though I'm certain Eric stares at me. If his focus could set me ablaze, I'd be roasting right now. I concentrate on Mr. McRae as he explains more about the job before unfortunately deferring to Eric for the specifics.

The actual interview process is a blur. When I stand as Mr. McRae and Eric thank me for my time, I worry I've bombed the interview. I don't even remember what was asked, much less how I answered.

"I'll walk you out," Eric offers.

"Don't take forever at lunch," Mr. McRae orders. "We have another interview at two."

Eric waves him off and I reluctantly follow him out of the room.

"I don't think I've seen you around town before. New to Cardinal Point?" he asks.

"I grew up here, but I haven't lived here for awhile."

He nods as if that makes sense. "Are you related to Robbie Stone?"

He knows my father? Why? How? Before I can answer, a blur collides into Eric. The blur is a woman who wraps her arms around him and kisses him in a way that should be inappropriate for the workplace. When she pulls away, my heart sinks. The brief hope that this is my Eric disappears. No way would he ever in a bazillion years date my horrible half-sister, Chelsea.

"I was thinking we could go to—"

"Chels, just a second. I was on my way to seeing Kate out." Eric looks a bit embarrassed, but that could be hopeful thinking.

Chelsea looks over at me and frowns. "You're back in town?" she asks me with a frown before turning to Eric, "Why is my sister here?"

"Half," I interrupt automatically. "Half sister."

Eric gives me a curious look before focusing back on Chelsea. While she interrogates him, I carefully yet casually step away and see myself out. This job sounded great, but working with someone whose judgment thinks it's a good idea to date my evil half-sister?

I'm not too sure anymore.

About the Author

Lindsay Paige is the author of multiple romances, most of which are set in the south. She dabbles in young adult, new adult, and sports romances. She also enjoys writing books with characters who deal with anxiety and depression, issues which are close to her heart. Lindsay lives in Alabama with her husband, daughter, and dog.

If you would like to hear news before anyone else, interact with Lindsay, and have a place to discuss her books with fellow fans, join Lindsay's League on Facebook. Be sure to sign up for her newsletter as well or visit her website: lindsaypaige.com

Also by Lindsay Paige

Cardinal Point series

Heaven and Hell Duet

Carolina Rebels series

Hearts in Carolina series

The Hourglass Duet

Sanity series

Bracing the Blue Line

Nepenthe

Without a Doubt

Bending Under Pressure

You Before Me

The Penalty Kill Trilogy

Oh Captain, My Captain series

The Ninth Inning series